"I must know the truth."

Armando's strong mouth twisted, but his tone was compassionate. "My housekeeper tells me you nearly fainted a while ago. It's clear she believes you're pregnant." His hand tightened over hers as she gasped in shock. "Are you, Pavane? Are you carrying my brother's child?"

Pavane knew what it must have cost her new husband to ask such a question. If she was pregnant, Armando would find himself tied to her for life. And she wanted to belong to him—skin to skin, heart to heart—but giving rein to her feelings for Armando would plunge her sister's marriage into jeopardy.

"No, Armando," she said passionately. "I swear it's quite impossible."

The tension left his face, and she felt a stab of pain that such a simple denial could bring him so much pleasure.

ANGELA WELLS left the bustling world of media marketing and advertising to marry and start a family in a suburb of London. Writing started out as a hobby, and she uses background she knows well from her many travels for her books. Her ambitions, she says, in addition to writing many more romances, are to visit Australia, pilot a light aircraft and own a word processing machine.

Sweet Poison

Angela Wells

Harlequin Books

TORONTO • NEW YORK • LONDON
AMSTERDAM • PARIS • SYDNEY • HAMBURG
STOCKHOLM • ATHENS • TOKYO • MILAN

Original hardcover edition published in 1986
by Mills & Boon Limited

ISBN 0-373-02790-7

Harlequin Romance first edition September 1986

Sin duda, que tus ojos
tinen veneno,
Desde que me miraste,
Me estoy muriendo.

Without doubt your eyes
hold poison,
Since the first look you gave me,
I know I die of love!

(Old Sevilian love song)

CHAPTER ONE

WHAT on earth *should* I do? Pavane gazed at the beautifully carved face of the Madonna as she asked her silent question.

Not that she expected an answer. Even if miracles did happen, her own short life had been totally devoid of them! Orphaned, with her sister, at the age of two—their talented parents both killed on a German autobahn when the coach carrying a famous London orchestra had crashed—her own embryonic career as a musician had been halted when her father's aunt—her guardian and only relative in England—had died a few months previously.

The comfort and style of her present existence she owed entirely to the generosity of her sister's husband, Rodrigo Valmontez, and of course, to Melody herself who, when it was clear she was destitute, had implored Rodrigo to offer his sister-in-law a home in Southern Spain where he owned a flourishing vineyard.

At first the shock and grief of Aunt Elaine's death had dominated Pavane's thoughts. It was only after the funeral that she had looked at her own future with equal amounts of courage and trepidation, wondering how she was going to support herself in an economic climate which offered little scope for unqualified musicians who were barely twenty years of age.

Another few months and she would have sat for her degree. Another year and she would have taken her Teacher's Diploma to open a wider field for her talents. As it was, her years of study without the final accolade of a degree made her a poor prospect for employment.

As soon as she had realised the size of the outstanding debts against Aunt Elaine's estate she had known there was no chance of her being able to continue at college, so when Melody had begged her to go back to Spain with her, it had seemed the perfect answer. It still was, if only ... A shaft of brilliant sunshine falling through the rose window above the altar illuminated the statue's face, giving the effect of a smile playing across the perfectly chiselled mouth. Pavane eyed it disconsolately. If only she could be sure Melody wasn't heading for disaster!

The change in her sister was undeniable. Melody was more brittle, more edgy than she had ever been in England, acting with a false gaiety Pavane had found bewildering. It was only in the last few days she had begun to suspect the reason. Each Sunday, when she and her sister had gone to church, they had been accompanied back to the vineyard by their neighbour's young brother; and Perico was a handsome young man, charming and polite. It was only natural, she had argued to herself, that Melody should like him, but this last Sunday the atmosphere between him and her sister had been charged with a heady emotion. To Pavane's sensitive perception it had screamed of an intimacy way beyond the normal level of friendship. It had come to her then, with startling clarity, that Melody was deeply involved emotionally with the young Spaniard!

For the last few days she had tossed the possibility over and over in her mind. If her suspicions were correct how long would it be before Rodrigo grew suspicious too? Quite apart from any other consideration, if Melody was having an affair, she was playing a dangerous game and one that could end in tragedy.

Pavane stared unseeingly at the carved wooden robes of the statue. On the other hand, if she had misread the signals she'd seen, would Melody ever forgive her if she confronted her? The last thing in the world she wanted to do was to offend or alienate her sister.

She sighed heavily, the sound breaking the silence of the deserted church. She had left Melody enjoying the customary siesta to walk slowly and aimlessly from the vineyard to the village, trying to come to terms with the problem. She hadn't intended to enter the church, but its cool interior had proved a welcome sanctuary from the shimmering heat of the dusty streets of Campos Altos. How hot and tired she felt in her simple blue cotton dress. Worse still, the walk hadn't cleared her mind at all. She still didn't know what action, if any, she should take!

'What should I *do*!' This time she spoke aloud, her irritation at her own inability to reach a solution making the question sound like a challenge.

'Ignore your heart and follow your conscience!'

Pavane spun round with a little scream of shock escaping her throat as her question was answered by an indisputably male voice in the same language as she had asked it. Her heart was pounding with surprised reaction as she sought to identify the source of the words in the dimness of the interior. The exhortation had certainly been highly moral—but it hadn't been Father Gomez who had made it. Of that she was positive.

As her eyes widened in an effort to locate the speaker, he moved from the shadows and she found herself gazing into the dark eyes of a stranger, catching her breath a little as she registered the full impact of his appearance. From the thick black hair that capped his well-shaped head, past the long straight nose to a mouth of sensuous, curving beauty, his face proclaimed a heritage from Moorish Spain.

Informally dressed, the immaculate cut of close-fitting dark trousers emphasised his lean tall figure: well over six feet in height, Pavane hazarded as she lifted her eyes to meet his, noting on the way how lovingly his well-tailored black shirt followed the line of athletically muscular shoulders.

She moved uneasily, aware that he was regarding her with a cool appraisal that had brought a guilty flush to her cheeks. Whatever must he be thinking of her—apparently addressing a statue like that! And if he *had* thought her plea sincere, how dared he take it upon himself to answer it! If he had been a young man and she had been anywhere else she might have thought he was trying to pick her up, figuratively speaking: but here in the village of Campos Altos the young men treated her with a reserve and courtesy that was far removed from that shown to foreigners on the beaches of the Costa del Sol. Besides, as the sister-in-law of Rodrigo Valmontez Pavane had found herself regarded with a respect bordering on awe during the past few weeks.

But this was no gauche young man flaunting his Spanish charm to flirt with an unknown blonde. As he moved a few steps closer to her, Pavane recognised the sophisticated maturity of a man in his early thirties: sensed a composure and authority in his bearing that had a tinge of hostility in it. Unexpectedly she shivered beneath his pensive gaze, immediately feeling even more foolish as his eyebrows lifted sardonically above eyes the colour of the midnight sea.

'Forgive me if, by speaking to you without introduction, I've offended you.' The words were humble, but nothing echoed their apology on the haughty, unsmiling face. He lifted a lazy hand towards the statue Pavane had been studying. 'I thought with such a chaperon I might dare approach you without causing you fear.'

So her shiver hadn't gone unnoticed! There had been a mocking edge to the speaker's voice and she had a strange feeling that to cause her disquiet was exactly what this enigmatic man *had* intended.

'Or perhaps it's my advice that offends you, hmm?'
The slightly supercilious twitch of his strong mouth
made her fingers curl into her palms in protest.

'If I am affronted, *señor*,' she told him sternly,
lifting her chin proudly, 'it would be because you saw
fit to preach to me about a matter which doesn't
concern you and about which you know nothing!'

He didn't like the rebuke, she noted with
satisfaction. Probably no woman in his household
dared to speak to him in such a manner. She
repressed the smile the thought invoked; there was no
point in antagonising him needlessly.

He shrugged expressive shoulders. 'You sounded
desperate. The advice was unquestionably good, and
certainly more than you could have received from a
wooden statue—however beautiful!'

'Yes, she is beautiful, exceedingly so!' Pavane
decided to ignore his attempt to rile her, her genuine
admiration for the carving overcoming her irritation.
'So different from the usual plaster saints.'

He nodded. 'Less pretty, I think. Less like a china
doll is our *Madonna do olivo*.'

'It is olive wood, then. I thought so!' Pavane had
identified the polished lines with their beautiful
graining accurately. 'Was it carved by a local man, do
you know?'

'Uh-huh.' He met her eyes, brimming with interest,
with a strange secretive smile. 'The artist lived in
these parts some sixty years ago. The story goes that
he carved the Madonna in the likeness of the woman
he loved above all other.'

Pavane allowed her eyes to drift back to the
exquisite olive wood features, seeing in their perfection
the devotion of the man who had fashioned them.

'How romantic!' she breathed. 'And how proud his
wife must have been.' Out of the corner of her eye she
glimpsed the sardonic lift of his expressive eyebrows

and felt herself blush at her own ingenuousness. 'It *was* his wife you meant?'

'His mistress, actually.' Dark Latin eyes dwelt on the fair-skinned, youthful face before him. 'His wife was many years his senior and so ugly she never had a picture taken or a portrait painted. Legend has it that she kept her face continually veiled.'

'Oh!' Her eyes dropped before the burning cynicism of his dark glance.

'I've often wondered,' he mused as if to himself, 'what motivated him to carve the face of his mistress on such a statue and offer it to the church. Was it meant as an insult to his wife, or to God—or both, perhaps?'

'Perhaps it was just his way of showing her how much he loved her,' she suggested quietly.

'Then he would have done better to carve the Magdalena rather than the Virgin Queen of Heaven!' The answer shook her with the depth of its asperity.

Her startled gaze lingered on the sharp, sculptured lines of his arrogant face, finding such unbending rectitude a little hard to take. 'I'm sure your moral attitude does you credit, *señor*, but it would appear the church took a more lenient view when they accepted the work.'

Even as his thick brows drew together in a frown of displeasure at her retort, Pavane was distracted by a low chuckle, feeling a sense of relief as Father Gomez entered from the vestry.

'I never thought to hear you on the receiving end of a lecture on charity, Armando!' His eyes twinkled with affection as they swept an amused glance between the two of them. He spoke in Spanish, but it was clear he had understood their conversation.

When Melody had become engaged to Rodrigo, Pavane had gone with her to extra coaching lessons in Spanish, and she was delighted now that she had no difficulty in speaking or understanding the language.

'Neither,' the priest continued, 'did I expect to find your presence gracing my humble church, my sòn! Particularly outside the hours of Mass—although your attendance these past few Sundays hasn't gone unremarked!'

Armando, as the priest had named him, rubbed a lean hand contemplatively down the side of his smooth jawline, as if considering his answer, his face eventually breaking into a rueful smile which lent an unexpected charm to his stern features. 'The truth of that,' he admitted after a pause, 'is that during the past few weeks my brother Rico has become so unusually devout that I was intrigued to discover the reason.'

'Ah, Rico . . .' The priest nodded his head as Pavane's heart gave an alarming lurch. 'Perhaps the more he studies the frailties of the human body in his medical books, the more he becomes aware of the importance of its soul?'

'Perhaps.' Armando's reply was polite, but the curl of his lips denied the explanation. 'Somehow I doubt it, though,' he finished drily. 'Although I'm sure my brother has a very good understanding of physical frailty.'

'Well, each man may seek God in his own way and for his own reason, my son.' There was a quiet, guarded look on Father Gomez's face.

'If indeed it is *God* whom my brother seeks!'

A slow smile curved the priest's mouth. 'There are many ways to God, are there not? And not all of them are dry and stony!' He looked again from Pavane's still face back to the dark-haired man at her side. 'The *señorita* is right: we should leave God to judge the motives of Miguel de Montilla!'

'Montilla?' Pavane interposed as the name registered. The same name that had been tormenting her thoughts all day! 'That's the name of our neighbours, isn't it?' She looked at the priest. 'I know Perico de

Montilla. Is the man who carved the statue a relation of his?'

'His grandfather.' It was Armando who answered, turning to face her, an expression of mocking amusement gleaming in the darkness of his deep-set eyes. 'Or should I say *our* grandfather?'

'Oh no!' There was quiet horror in the words that escaped her. Melody had told her Perico was the youngest of three brothers, the eldest of whom owned the adjoining land to the vineyard. 'You're Perry's brother!' she exclaimed, her mind busily evaluating the comments he had just made. 'I'm sorry—I'd no idea. I'm Pavane Calvadene. My sister is Melody Valmontez.'

Armando nodded his head slightly. 'I know who you are, *señorita*. I would hardly have spoken to you otherwise.'

Pavane felt the rebuff in his voice. How dared he fault her for replying to him because they hadn't been introduced! He must have known it had been merely out of politeness. It was a pity she hadn't snubbed him completely! Feeling the flush of annoyance rise to her cheeks, she made to turn away, freezing as his hand detained her.

'I am, as you say, Rico's brother,' he continued gravely, 'Armando de Montilla y Cabra.'

To her surprise he lifted her hand to his lips, his mouth brushing warm and dry against the soft skin in a salutation which was as contrived to her fancy as it appeared gallant. She could see from the priest's face that he found the tableau amusing, probably diverted by her wide-eyed reaction which lacked Latin sophistication.

'What a splendid name,' she murmured languidly, determined not to be outfaced by such outrageous smoothness, 'It reminds me of rich wine and rich men. You're not going to surprise me further by telling me you're really a nobleman in disguise?'

'You don't know?' Hidden laughter lent a strange masculine beauty to the lean planes of his Moorish face. 'My house is known locally as *El Cortijo del Rey*.'

Caught up in a game of words, Pavane momentarily pushed to the back of her mind the threat that this man's presence here in the church posed her. 'The King's Farm!' she translated delightedly. 'Now a *marqués* or a *conde* I might have accepted—but a king!' Her mischievous face assumed an expression of awe. 'To what throne do you aspire, I wonder, *señor*?'

'Alas, it's the farm that has the title, not I. I aspire to nothing more than being a competent farmer.'

A farmer indeed! At least he hadn't said 'a simple farmer'! She must ask Melody to tell her more about the vast Montilla estates that bordered the Valmontez land. It would be interesting to find out just what Armando's definition of 'farmer' was.

He released her hand. 'Perhaps now you've received the answer to your prayer, you would allow me to drive you back home, *señorita*?' There was a moment's hesitation. 'That is, of course, if you're satisfied you *have* received an answer?'

Pavane stared at him, hating the cynical twist that distorted the strong masculine mouth, and experiencing a sense of despair as Father Gomez, after bestowing a benign smile on both of them, continued his passage down the aisle towards the main door.

There was no doubt in her mind that Armando had suspected all along that his brother was indulging in an affair, she realised bitterly. He had all but said so to the priest! And she had actually accused him of interfering in something which didn't concern him!

'You followed me in here!' she accused him, angry with herself that his presence should make her feel so unbearably guilty.

He shrugged with Latin grace. 'The church's doors are always open to all who seek her comfort, but yes, since you ask, I did see you enter. Such devotion impressed me.'

She didn't have to be a mind-reader to know he'd meant 'astounded' him. Carefully, because she was about to tread on very thin ice, she drew in a long breath. 'Your brother, Perico, is twenty-three years of age . . .' she began.

'Still at university, immature, impulsive and with a tendency to bring disaster down upon his head!' he finished her sentence succinctly.

'Then it is your brother to whom you should speak,' Pavane told him curtly.

'Believe me, I intend to now. Your attitude convinces me I've not been mistaken in my observations. At the same time, *señorita*, I should like to think I might have your co-operation.' There was a cold hauteur in the narrowed eyes. 'You know nothing can come of such a liaison!'

Pavane gave a brief humourless laugh. Of course she knew! 'Ignore my heart and follow my conscience, you mean?'

'It would be in everybody's interests,' he agreed, watching her intently.

Perhaps God did work in mysterious ways His wonders to perform, she thought a trifle hysterically, and Armando had been used as a mouthpiece from on high. Although to her jaundiced eye, he looked more like the Dark Angel than Gabriel! One thing she didn't doubt: he would wield tremendous power over the pleasant, youthful Perico. The hierarchy of Spanish families worked like that. Also, of course, he had right on his side—the affair had been doomed from the first day!

'If—if I do,' she asked a little tremulously, as the memory of Melody's strained face floated across her mind's eye, 'can I depend on you to be discreet?'

'Ah . . .' He had sensed her compliance, and quiet

satisfaction lent a subtle charm to his prepossessing face. 'Promise me you'll put an end to this relationship and I swear no one will ever be any the wiser!'

CHAPTER TWO

'He knows, Melly. Armando de Montilla knows his brother's formed an ... an attachment to you!' Pavane gazed anxiously at her sister's ashen face. 'Oh, Melly, I guessed it myself a few days ago, but I didn't want to believe it!' Her hands moved nervously together. 'I don't know how I would have survived these past months without your generosity. The last thing I wanted to do was to interfere, but it's so terribly, terribly wrong what you're doing ... Oh, Melly—why?'

'I don't see how he can know.' Melody raised stricken blue eyes to stare at her sister's concerned face. 'Perry would never betray me. We've been so discreet ...'

'I know. And I don't suppose anyone who wasn't close to either of you would notice. It was some time before I realised you'd been using the Sunday morning service to arrange rendezvous for when Rodrigo was away from home. It was only when I saw the way you looked at each other that it dawned on me—that and a dozen other small things. It all began to add up. Armando's been going to the church especially to watch Perico. He must have seen it too.'

'But why should Armando speak to *you* about it?' Once Melody had been beautiful, now her face seemed gaunt and lined. She was only a few years older than Pavane yet in appearance there might have been a decade between the two women at that moment.

'He followed me into the church. We were alone there, and I suppose he saw it as a good opportunity to advise me to warn you that he intends to put an end to it.'

'He's going to tell Rodrigo!' Fear flecked Melody's azure eyes with a glittering panic. 'He'll kill me, Pavane. Oh, God—you don't know what it's been like living with him these last months!'

'Armando promised he wouldn't do that.' Pavane regarded her sister with grave concern. 'But I don't understand. You were head-over-heels in love with Rodrigo when you married. However could you do this to him?'

Arriving at the Valmontez estate, Pavane had been aware immediately of the coolness between her sister and brother-in-law, but had been too polite to mention it. At the back of her mind had been the haunting fear that she herself might have been the cause of it. Perhaps Rodrigo hadn't wanted to shoulder the burden of his wife's young sister? She knew how close family ties were in Spain, but she had shied from the idea of having to accept charity without affection. Now she waited with bated breath in case Melody was about to confirm her suspicions.

'We quarrelled because he found out I was taking the Pill,' Melody said bleakly. 'He was furious. He accused me of not loving him ... not wanting to have his child ... of—of sleeping with other men, which of course I wasn't ... not then ...' Her voice broke.

'You can get the Pill over here?' Surprised, for a moment, Pavane was diverted from the main issue.

Melody made a gesture in which despair was mixed with resignation. 'I brought a supply with me from England when I first came here. Afterwards I discovered they could be bought over the counter at certain pharmacists at the popular resorts. Oh, they're not advertised for that purpose and they're not prescribed, but once you know the brand name it's easy!' She gave a harsh laugh. 'Spain is changing, Pavvy. It's two different worlds now—the old traditional and the new contemporary. Unfortunately for me, Rodrigo belongs to the old one.'

'But Melly, you always wanted to have children . . .' Pavane shook her golden head in wonderment. 'I still don't understand.'

'I was so young when I married—too young really. All I saw was the glamour and romance. I was infatuated with Rodrigo. I wanted to be with him all the time, but he was away so much on business and I was lonely and homesick. Don't you see, Pavvy? I wanted to get used to living here before I started to raise a family.' Her voice thickened with tears. 'When he found out, I couldn't make him see my point of view. He called me the most dreadful names, and then he said he wished he'd never married me!'

'Oh, dear God . . .' Pavane's face was nearly as white as the older girl's, but Melody brushed her exclamation away.

'He still makes love to me, if you could call it that— without care or tenderness or consideration. Nothing matters except his own driving needs.' She choked on a sob. 'We might just as well have a pillow down the bed between us afterwards. He never touches me— never.'

'And Perico?' Pavane asked gently, moved despite her horror by the obvious depth of Melody's distress.

'It started as a friendship. We used to walk back from church together. Rodrigo never goes, but it made an excuse for me to get away from the atmosphere of the house. It wasn't until some time later I discovered Perico only went because he'd seen me going in alone and he was—interested.' Her slim fingers entwined, betraying her strain. 'He was on holiday from medical school and he was bored . . .'

'And he was handsome, kind and understanding,' Pavane supplied with resigned comprehension.

Melody nodded. 'All of those things, but he was also

a man: young, passionate, wanting to love and be loved. So . . .' She raised her wan countenance to Pavane's. 'I couldn't talk to the priest, but I could talk to Perico.' She buried her face in her hands as Pavane recoiled from the deep sobs that racked her sister's slender body. 'The dreadful thing is, I still love Rodrigo! If there was any way, any way at all I could make him love me again—do you think I wouldn't take it?'

'But you and Perico are . . . are lovers?' Desperately Pavane still clung to a thread of hope that the emotional closeness had stopped short of actual physical involvement. But one look at Melody's face and the hope withered and died. It was every bit as bad as she'd feared; the ramifications terrifying. 'Dear Heaven, Melody,' she cried, 'suppose you conceived a child!'

'Don't worry, that's impossible.' For a moment Melody's eyes slid away from Pavane's accusing gaze, to return a few seconds later burning with an angry defiance. 'I promise you I'll never have a baby unless it's Rodrigo's—and only then if by some miracle he looks at me with love once more.'

Melody's behaviour was certainly bizarre, Pavane thought wretchedly as she watched her sister cry. Perhaps she was on the edge of a complete breakdown? As for Perico—what he'd done was inexcusable. In her heart she could fully understand how appalled Armando must have been when he had first suspected what was going on.

She put a remonstrative hand on Melody's shoulder. 'It's got to end,' she said firmly. 'For everyone's sake, you've got to put a stop to it. Can't you see how wrong it is?' A wave of pity overcame her as Melody's face seemed to crumple before her eyes, but she forced herself to be stern.

For years Melody had been the centre of attention,

spoiled because of her natural beauty and affectionate character. She had drifted through life being everyone's darling, and the first real test had left her wanting.

If only her sister had confided in Rodrigo from the start about the way she felt ... Remembering his ardent devotion to her sister in London, Pavane felt sure that with a little tact she could have made him understand. But this ...

'Yes, I know.' Melody dabbed at her eyes with a tissue. 'If only I'd realised the extent of Rodrigo's personal pride before I married him, I might have coped better—now I can't reach him.' She tried to smile, her trembling mouth only succeeding in a wry twist. 'Let it be a warning to you, Pavvy. Never fall in love with an Andalusian! They're volatile, graceful, charming and ardent lovers—but they make deadly enemies.' Her voice shook. 'And they can break a woman's heart with impossible cruelty.'

Pavane watched, eyes darkened with shock and anxiety as her sister rose to her feet. 'I was going to finish it anyway,' Melody whispered. 'I don't love Perico, I know that. I think he's fond of me and he finds me attractive ...' She turned away, unable to meet Pavane's clear-eyed sorrow. 'It's different now I've got you, Pavvy. You can't imagine how I've longed to be able to speak English again with someone. If only you'd been here at the start, then maybe none of this would have happened.'

The memory of Armando de Montilla's haughty condemnation of his grandfather and the priest's gentle reproof about offering judgment surged into Pavane's mind. 'It's not that I don't appreciate how you must feel ...' she began hesitantly.

'Oh, but you don't!' For the first time there was a subdued anger in Melody's voice. 'How can you possibly understand?' She gave a harsh raw laugh.

'That saying—it's better to have loved and lost than never to have loved at all. Believe me, it's a lie! Nothing, *nothing* can possibly be worse than loving a man, wanting to feel him possess you with tenderness and affection, only to find yourself used and rejected!' Her tear-washed eyes softened as she gazed at Pavane's still face. 'I pray to God *you* never know what it's like to be in love and have that love thrown back in your face!'

For a moment she raised her eyes blazing with pain to meet Pavane's. Her pride stripped bare, she challenged Pavane's condemnation.

For a moment the younger girl hesitated, aware of her own inexperience of men, of loving, but she had to tell the truth as she saw it. 'What you're doing isn't the answer. It can only destroy what still exists between you and your husband. You have to see that, Melody.'

'Yes, I see it.' The subdued tone wrenched at Pavane's heart. 'I'll put an end to it immediately, I promise you.'

It was a long time before Pavane could sleep that night, and when she finally drifted to a light unconsciousness, her rest was broken by colourful and disturbing dreams. Awakening suddenly, her heart pounding ferociously, she shot up in bed listening. Surely something had broken the veil of sleep?

Moonlight lay across her bed in silver fingers and the air was filled with the sweet scent of peppery carnations and ripening oranges—a smell as typical of Andalusia as the flamenco and fighting bulls for which it was renowned.

Pavane put her hand against the thudding pulse in her chest. Her skin felt warm and clammy. Her eyes were fast growing accustomed to the moonlit room and there was no need to turn the light on as she reached to her bedside table to find the atomiser of cologne which had been a parting gift from her boy-friend Kevin. She sprayed the cool perfume on her throat and arms, letting its coolness trickle down the slopes of her full breasts beneath the filmy broderie anglaise nightdress she wore.

Kevin had been a dear friend, she thought with happy reflection, but that had been all. She had never been tempted to fall in love with him—never.

Fearing that sleep would continue to elude her, she swung her slim, shapely legs out of bed and padded to the window, opening the wooden shutter so she could gaze down on the patio.

For the rest of her life she would wonder what quirk of fate drew her to the window at precisely that moment.

In the stillness of the Spanish night, the first pale movement at the far side of the patio caught and held her attention, her hands gripping the windowsill as the blur of movement solidified with nearness and she recognised Melody's fair head, the shocking pink of her cardigan, and the white dress she had worn at dinner. Melody was running towards the house as if every devil from Hell was in her wake. Pavane felt a cold trickle of fear trace the line of her own spine. Something was terribly wrong!

Not troubling to stop and collect a wrap or even to slip her feet into shoes, she darted from the bedroom, taking the stairs in the long sweeping staircase two at a time in her hurry: speeding along the cool stone-paved hall, reaching the front door as it opened and Melody half fell into the house.

Pavane saw at once that her sister was in a state of shock. Her face was pallid, her mouth opening and shutting without sound, her eyes wide and staring. She grabbed Melody's arms, steadying her, holding her closely, feeling the elder girl's deep shuddering convulsions.

'Melly darling, what is it? What's happened? For God's sake tell me!'

'Rodrigo. Rodrigo saw us.' Melody's voice was a thin thread of fear. 'I'd already arranged to meet Perry tonight because Rodrigo was supposed to be staying in Seville. I told him it was over between us.' She was shaking so much that Pavane was half-supporting her, feeling her sister's terror seeping into her own bones. 'He wouldn't believe me. He thought I was teasing . . .'

'He forced himself on you?' The horror in Pavane's voice seemed to stabilise Melody an instant.

'No, oh no. Not like you mean. He—he was persuasive. He begged to love me just one more time. He seemed so stunned, I couldn't find the heart to say no. We—we were making love and I opened my eyes. I saw him, Pavvy. I saw my husband the other side of the patio. He was watching us—just standing there watching us.'

Fighting down her own rising panic, Pavane forced her question through bone-dry lips. 'What happened?'

It was a question she hardly dared to ask, her eyes going to the front door swinging gently on its hinges, expecting Rodrigo to erupt into the house at any moment.

'I ran,' Melody whispered. 'I cried out to Perry and I pushed him away—and I ran . . .'

She clung desperately to the younger girl. 'It's the end for me, Pavvy. If Rodrigo doesn't actually kill me he'll make my life an unending hell. Oh, God, what am I going to do!'

What indeed! Shocked and angry as she was at Melody's weakness and the way in which she had broken her promise, Pavane knew it was no time to lecture her.

'I'll do what I can,' she said quietly. Even as she said it she knew it was a vain offer. What could she do to mitigate Rodrigo's justifiable fury? She shuddered, imagining the consequences for her sister.

'Pavvy!' Melody's fingers bit into her shoulders. 'Perry's out there with him. He'll murder him!' She was half-fainting with sheer terror.

Pavane bit her lip thoughtfully. For all their drama there was probably a lot of truth in Melody's words. If the two men had come to blows what chance would the graceful, slender Perico have against the strength and power of the older man he had wronged?

Whatever the moral rights Pavane winced at the thought of the damage her brother-in-law could wreak on that handsome youthful face of the man who had dared to dishonour his wife. Besides, he might even kill him! That would be a tragedy which would affect many lives—not least of all Rodrigo's own.

She would have to try to stop him.

'Listen to me, Melly,' she said sternly, assuming a confidence she was far from feeling. 'I'm going to try and stop them fighting.'

'All right,' Melody agreed as if in a trance, 'but you can't go out like that.' Her eyes fastened on the openworked embroidery of Pavane's nightdress where the pink thrust of her breasts was clearly visible. 'Here, take my jacket.' She hung her cardigan over Pavane's shoulders. 'And wear my mules.' She stepped out of the wedged sandals, allowing Pavane to slide her feet into them. 'And for pity's sake hurry!'

Pavane needed no further encouragement, running across to the orange grove, her feet speeding over the white paved patio, her heart pounding a desperate beat as she anticipated what she might find, her hands clutching the flimsy cardigan round her shoulders.

At first she could make out nothing between the darkness of the trees. Then she heard the noise of bone thudding against flesh and saw them, her hand instinctively rising to her mouth in horror.

'No!' she screamed. 'Stop it! Oh, stop it, I beg you!'

As she drew nearer she saw the two figures, which had been locked together in combat, part: saw the younger, more slender one drop to the ground.

Perico lay face downward on the grass beneath the trees, his knees drawn up, his right arm beneath his chest, the left arm cradled across the top of his dark head. It was a pitiful attitude of defeat that brought the tears starting to her eyes. However much he had deserved retribution, she could still feel sorry for him.

Rodrigo was standing staring at her, his face in shadow, his powerful body tensed. From the distance between them she couldn't see whether he had been hurt or not, but he looked every inch the victor.

'So you came back to plead for him, did you?' Rodrigo's voice, heavy with emotion, thrust through the still atmosphere. To Pavane's horror he lifted his boot and thrust it against Perico's chest so he turned on his back. He stirred slightly, as she realised with a sickening dread that he was quite defenceless.

Transfixed to the spot, hardly aware of the words Rodrigo had spoken, she pleaded again. 'He's had enough—leave him.'

'Enough? Not yet!' There was no humour in the knowing laugh that echoed from Rodrigo's throat. 'You returned just in time, *querida*, to see your lover reap the results of his daring.'

Another movement as his foot straightened Perry's bent legs, leaving the young man's body totally unprotected. 'By the time I've finished with him, not only will he never make love to another man's wife— he'll never make love to any woman as long as he lives!'

He moved a couple of strides, bent and straightened up. Pavane's knees went weak as the blood drained from her face. Rodrigo was holding a riding crop and she realised the dreadful revenge he intended to extort.

Words were no longer of use. Only action was possible. As Rodrigo swung his arm back, she darted forward towards Perico's body spreadeagled on the ground—and it was then she saw the solution as clearly as if a light had been switched on in a cellar.

Rodrigo had called her *querida*. He had taunted her with 'coming back'. Rodrigo thought *she* was Melody! If he could make that mistake across the distance they had just faced, she could bluff him into believing Melody's innocence.

Her sister had said he had stood the other side of the patio watching. He had seen a blonde head, a white dress, a pink cardigan, but he hadn't identified her beyond all possible doubt. With one simple lie she could give Melody the chance to save her marriage, stop Rodrigo from committing an act which could send him to jail and save Perico from an unspeakable punishment. Rodrigo might want to emasculate his wife's lover, but he would hardly extort such retribution on his sister-in-law's behalf however much he might disapprove of her behaviour.

Even as Rodrigo hesitated, Pavane flung herself protectively between Perico and her brother-in-law, turning her face towards his threatening presence.

'It was me!' she cried. 'It was me you saw, Rodrigo, not Melody. Perico's my lover . . . mine!'

She heard him swear: saw the hand drop limply to his side as the crop fell back to the ground. Then she was kneeling over the body of the young Spaniard, her face drained of colour as she took in his swollen mouth, the grazed cheek, the cut above one sleek eyebrow. Either Perico had been hopelessly outclassed or in his guilt he had chosen to accept a measure of the penalty he deserved. She shuddered, remembering just how extreme that penalty could have been but for her interference.

Even as she watched, his eyelids flickered and he

struggled to sit upright. It was essential he know what she had done. Her voice was soft and urgent, trying to pierce the fog of concussion he was fighting.

'Perry ... *querido* ...' She swallowed, her voice gaining strength. '*Querido*, listen to me, it's Pavane. Can you hear me? Do you understand? Rodrigo thought it was Melody out here with you. But I've told him the truth. I've told him it was me, Pavane.'

'Pavane.' He spoke her name through bruised and swollen lips.

'That's right,' she said, seeing the intelligence taking over from the emptiness that had cloaked his dark eyes. 'He knows it wasn't Melody. He knows it was you and me.'

'Oh, *Dios*!' There was a wealth of meaning in the words as he clutched his ribs, pain clearly written on his damaged face.

She helped him to sit upright, stiffening as his head lolled forward against her own soft breasts. She raised steady eyes to meet Rodrigo's stern regard. His anger, she saw with a sense of relief, had drained away, but there was no forgiveness or understanding on his cold face.

He moved towards her, taking her arm, and she allowed him to separate her from Perico, rising to her feet at his command.

'You'd better go back to the house,' he said curtly. 'Wake Melody and tell her what's happened.' His gaze never wavered. 'Explain I came back unexpectedly from Seville and seeing movements in the orange grove stopped to investigate.' He stared at her pallid face. 'Then you'd better go to bed—I'll speak to you in the morning.'

It was the opportunity Pavane needed to tell Melody what she had done. Whatever the consequences, they would be less serious for her than for her sister.

Melody was no hard-eyed, conniving *femme fatale*, taking pleasure in deceiving her husband. She was a deeply affectionate woman, warm and generous, seemingly spurned by the husband she truly wanted, and desperately if ill-advisedly seeking comfort from the nearest source that offered it.

She'd been a fool. But if her foolishness was going to mean the total destruction of her marriage, it was a high price to pay for her stupidity.

Besides, supposing Rodrigo raised his hand to her in anger? Perico's bruised face swam before her eyes, to be replaced in her imagination by the delicate, classical beauty of her sister, and she shuddered. No, she'd made the right decision. This way no one would be badly hurt.

A movement behind her made her turn to where Perico had struggled to his feet, still dazed and unsteady.

'Don't worry about your boyfriend!' Rodrigo laughed without humour. 'He's quite safe now. I'll drive him back to the Cortijo del Rey. They'll see he's patched up and delivered in one piece to his brother.

'Armando de Montilla will know exactly what has to be done now!'

CHAPTER THREE

'PAVANE, it's me, Melody.'

The gentle knock at her door preceded the entrance of her sister carrying a tray. Pavane, already dressed in jeans and a T-shirt, turned from the window. She had been too worried and scared to find refuge in sleep for any length of time the previous night, only the memory of the wonder and gratitude on her sister's face when she had told her what had happened had proved some consolation to her troubled spirit.

Despite Melody's half-hearted protestations, she had been adamant in refusing to retract her false admission, insisting Melody confirmed the story to Rodrigo when he returned from the Cortijo.

Had her sister been able to maintain the lie? she wondered. From the relatively composed appearance of the older girl, it seemed likely. Pavane smiled her relief.

'I thought we'd have breakfast here so we can talk.' Melody's hands shook as she placed her burden on the table.

'Was Rodrigo very angry when he came back?' Pavane couldn't keep the tremor from her voice.

'Not so much angry as . . . well . . . resigned. But he was relieved, too. He—he actually told me he suspected it was me at first. Oh God, Pavvy, you can't imagine how guilty I felt. I almost confessed and threw myself on his mercy, but—but . . .' Melody's voice trembled, 'he was so kind to me. I couldn't stop shaking and he assumed it was because I was so worried about what *you'd* done. He promised me it would be all right.' She gave a desperate little laugh.

'For the first time in months he put his arm round me and cuddled me!' She bit her lip, forcing back tears. 'He told me he loved me, had always loved me, but when he found out I was on the Pill he was so jealous because he thought I must have a lover and he was determined to find out who it was and—and kill him!'

It was a dreadful irony that there had been no lover and that Rodrigo's unbending attitude had brought one into existence!

Melody lifted a slim hand to dry the tears that had started to moisten her cheeks. 'I don't deserve a second chance, Pavvy—and certainly not at your expense—but heaven knows I *need* one, if only to prove to Rodrigo how much I love him—have always loved him!' Her voice broke poignantly. 'Last night when I couldn't sleep I listened to Rodrigo's steady breathing and I kept thinking—suppose he'd killed Perico? All the lives that would have been ruined because of me— because I was too weak to live with the responsibility of being married to a real man—tough, un-compromising, idealistic. . .' Tears flooded her cheeks. 'I never meant to hurt him like I have!'

Pavane sipped her coffee. Back home in England Melody with her advantage in years had always been the star. She had been the bright, beautiful ring-leader, always the centre of attraction, so that when Rodrigo had come to a vintners' conference and stayed at the hotel where she had been a receptionist, he had fallen desperately in love with her, wooing her with an ardour and a passion that had entranced her lovely sister.

It had been she, Pavane, who had always stood on the fringe of the action looking wistfully at her composed and elegant sister. Now the roles had been reversed and it was she who had to make the decisions and ensure Melody obeyed. If there was a chance that Melody's marriage could be mended, and from her

sister's penitent attitude there seemed every possibility
of it, surely the painful slur against her own morals
would be bearable?

Pavane sighed, suddenly feeling much older than
her twenty years. 'You have your second chance,
Melly. Leave things as they are. In a few days the
whole thing will be forgotten anyway.'

'Oh, Pavane! It won't be as easy as that! I was so
afraid you might not understand!'

'Understand what?' Surprise mantled Pavane's
pretty face, as Melody twisted the gold ring on her
finger.

'Last night when Rodrigo took Perry back to the
Cortijo he demanded to see Armando. He told him
what had happened. How he found you and Perry . . .'

'Yes?' Pavane felt the colour suffusing her face. Of
all the people to whom her supposed indiscretions had
to be imparted Armando was the last she would have
chosen. Self-righteous and cold, he would be appalled
and disgusted. Even if his opinion was of no value to
her, the thought of that scornful smile made her feel
sick. But Melody hadn't finished.

'He told him that the only possible outcome was
for Perry to marry you.'

'Marry!' Pavane didn't know whether to laugh or
cry. 'But that's absurd. I mean, even if we'd been
lovers it's still absurd! And Rodrigo is only my
brother-in-law, not my father.'

'You're living in his house and he's accepted
responsibility for you.'

'But Perry won't marry me! How could he? Oh,
don't worry, Melody. It's just a charade, isn't it? No
one can force Perry to ask me to marry him, and if he
did, no one can force me to accept!'

'Armando can force Perico,' Melody told her
quietly. 'He pays his fees and supports him entirely at
the university in Madrid. Besides, Perico would obey

Armando. He's not strong-willed enough to oppose him.'

'So all right.' Pavane admitted to herself the possibility of Armando forcing Perico's hand. 'It's known that English girls have more freedom in these matters. If Perry proposes I'll refuse him.' Her voice was brave but her eyes wary as she met her sister's gaze. 'There's no way Rodrigo can make me accept, is there?'

'No,' Melody acknowledged. 'But you'll probably find he and Armando will form a strong and formidable masculine threat. They're both intensely proud men.'

Pavane attempted a laugh. 'There'll be some way out—just give me time to think about it!'

'There isn't going to be a lot of time, I'm afraid.' Melody placed her hand over her sister's. 'Rodrigo told me to let you know he's taking you over to the Cortijo at ten this morning. Armando's asked to see you.'

'You mean he's already decided to force Perry to offer me marriage to save the honour of the Montilla y Cabras?' Pavane's small chin thrust out defiantly. 'I suppose he thinks I'll be humble and grateful. Well, I've got news for Don Armando. He can take his family honour and—and throw it in the arena for the bulls to trample! Nothing on earth will make me go into a loveless marriage with Perico—and that's what I intend to tell his brother!'

'Darling Pavvy . . .' Melody's hand tightened over hers. 'Are you sure you can go through with this?'

'Of course I can!' She wished she felt as confident as she knew she sounded. 'I'm not scared of Armando de Montilla!'

'This way, *señorita*. The *patrón* is expecting you.'

The manservant gave her a slight bow and she

followed him into the wide hallway, her eye immediately captured by the sweeping curve of the staircase leading from its cool confines.

'A moment, please.' He had taken her to the threshold of a large wooden door which he now opened. Looking over his shoulder, Pavane could make out a spacious room which appeared to be lined with amply filled bookshelves. On a large trestle table there was an assortment of papers, maps and diagrams and against the window wall stood a large desk copiously covered with what appeared to be bills, invoices, receipts and letters.

Her eyes were inevitably drawn to the figure seated behind the desk as the deep-set eyes of Armando, softened by the dark wealth of lashes that blurred their outline, were lifted from the work in front of him to sweep across her face.

He was speaking on the telephone, but the moment he saw her he rose to his feet, indicating that she enter and be seated on the chair facing him across the desk. He waited until she had complied before re-seating himself and continuing his conversation, which seemed to be about the price of fertilisers. In his other hand he held a pen poised dormant over a sheet of paper. It occurred to her that here was a man who didn't doodle designs while in conversation: a man who was controlled and careful not to betray what was on his mind. A formidable opponent!

But if his hand was still, his eyes certainly were not. Pavane felt herself flushing under the intensity of his stare as he took the opportunity of the silence between them to evaluate her appearance from top to toe.

Under the impertinence of that scrutiny, Pavane felt herself wilt, knowing all the shortcomings he would find. In the first place she had been too upset to care about trying to make an impression. True, she had darkened her fair brows and lashes, but her pale skin with its dusting of freckles had not even come to passing acquaintance with foundation or powder. Neither had she bothered to put on lipstick. As for her hair—well, there wasn't much she could have done about that anyway. Before she had left England she had had it cut to a length of two inches all over and lightly permed so that it clung in soft baby curls to her head. Long enough to cover the top of her ears and break the line of her forehead, but not long enough to be anything other than a mop!

As Armando's expressionless gaze strayed to her breasts, sharply outlined against the pale blue T-shirt that matched her eyes, she recalled it had been purchased in a sale, while the jeans that hugged her slim thighs had certainly known better days.

Until Armando had subjected her to this visual examination she hadn't even thought of her appearance. Now she wished she had.

At last he replaced the phone. 'I apologise for keeping you waiting. I've arranged for no more calls to be put through to me for the time being.'

Pavane nodded her head, silently accepting his apology, knowing it was merely a formality. She refused to be the first to speak. After all, he had invited her here. If he had something to say then he could say it. She stared at him, her eyes taking on a defiance of their own as she became aware of the quickened pulse in her own throat.

When she had first met Armando she hadn't known he was Perry's brother. Now she could see the family likeness. But what in Perry was a youthful attractiveness of dark eyes, firm skin and pleasant features, in Armando had matured to a strictly masculine beauty of hard bone and well-tuned muscle. That Perry was malleable she didn't doubt, for however attracted to Melody he had been, he should have had the willpower to adhere to the moral code of his culture.

Instead he had taken advantage of Melody's confessed unhappiness and loneliness. She doubted if Armando would ever be so self-indulgent as to make such a disastrous mistake. He would be a man in control of most things—his own emotions particularly. She found no comfort in the thought.

Now he leaned back in his large swivel chair, laying the pen down on the desk, stretching his long legs lazily.

'I must be frank with you, *señorita*. If you've come here with any hopes of marrying my brother, then you would be wise to forget them. My feelings have undergone no change since our conversation yesterday.'

His words were spoken in a businesslike manner, but Pavane caught the dark gleam of challenge behind his watchful face, and suddenly she knew. It had been *she* he had suspected all the time—not Melody at all! She coloured furiously at the realisation, but at least that made the part she was playing easier. Her embarrassment was followed by a wave of relief. Thank heavens Armando understood. An enforced marriage with Perico would have been ludicrous!

'How is Perry?' she asked him with quiet concern.

'Feeling very sorry for himself when he left for Madrid early this morning.' Dark, amused eyes taunted her. 'I imagine his face will heal in time, but I fancy his ribs will pain him for a while yet.'

So Perry had been sent away. Apparently Armando had decided their relationship was to be terminated forthwith. The memories of Perry's injuries brought a quick frown to her face and she winced, knowing how very much worse they could have been.

At the movement Armando's eyebrows rose in assumed surprise. 'You didn't believe your behaviour would draw down its own retribution?' His lips curled disbelievingly. 'It appears *your* fortune to have emerged unscathed, *señorita*. Perhaps because you are unaware of the standards we demand from our women, you were treated more leniently.'

'My only punishment has been to be forced to visit you, *señor*,' she retorted tartly, stung by his criticism. 'Although I can't guess for what purpose.'

'Can't you?' His gaze was openly mocking. 'Then I'll tell you. Your brother-in-law has withdrawn his protection from you. He's made it quite clear to me that in his opinion you've forfeited any right to remain as part of his family unit.'

Rodrigo meant to turn her out! She'd have to find the means of fending for herself. Pavane sucked in her breath, refusing to let the supercilious man sitting in front of her see just how frightening she found that prospect.

Of course she had never intended to live off Rodrigo's bounty for ever! Although at the time her brother-in-law had made it very clear that he accepted full and total responsibility for her welfare while she was under his roof. No, once she had settled down she had intended to look around to find gainful employment. If not in her chosen field of music—well, she was young and healthy with fluent Spanish and she had been certain she would find something else given time! What she hadn't anticipated was the immediacy of the decision she must make. Quickly she gathered her thoughts together.

'Why should he need *you* to tell me that?' she asked proudly. 'Is my sin so great he can't even bring himself to speak to me?'

For a moment she fancied his glance softened and she prayed he hadn't noticed the betraying glitter of tears in her eyes.

'He's disturbed by what took place, naturally.' His tone was still noncommittal. 'He demands that my brother fulfils his obligations to you.'

'Makes an honest woman of me?' Pavane laughed at the hackneyed phrase. 'But you've other plans for Perry, as you've just told me, so there's no point in this interview. I'm not in the mood for lectures!' She rose to her feet as she spoke.

'Pavane! Wait.' It was the first time Armando had spoken her name and the sound of it on his tongue shocked her. 'Sit down.'

She stood staring at him. He had sprung to his feet as quickly as she, and now stood in silhouette against the sun-filled window. His powerful presence seemed to dominate the office and she was acutely aware of his brown skin against the white rolled-up sleeves of his shirt, the vee of flesh at his neck, his strong slender hands splayed out on the desk before him.

'Please,' he added.

There was such authority in his voice that she obeyed him, taking possession of the chair, sitting meekly with legs together, her hands in her lap.

Seeing her settled, he subsided slowly into his own chair.

'My decision sounds hard to you, I realise that.' He paused and she made no effort to deny his statement. If she had been truly involved, if she had loved Perry, then yes, his decision would have been unbearably harsh. His narrowed eyes registered something of the mute defiance on her face and she saw his mouth tighten. 'My brother has another four years before he can qualify as a doctor. As I tried to make you see yesterday, there's no way he can take on the responsibilities of a wife and a possible family within that time and still hope to achieve his ambitions. In any case,' and now there was a decided chill to his voice, 'he's far too young and immature to tie himself down to one woman. Too many marriages fail because they are contracted when the partners, particularly the man, are too young.'

Privately Pavane agreed with him, but she had no intention of saying so. 'You speak from experience?' she dared to ask.

'From observation,' Armando bit back. 'It's my intention to preserve Rico from that! On the other hand, he is partially to blame for your predicament, and since I've prevented him from making reparation in the accepted way, I must accept some of that responsibility.'

Did he know how pompous he sounded? she wondered. Or was it the way he was translating the Spanish into English for her? The last person she needed to take responsibility for her was this self-designated farmer who looked more like a Spanish Grandee with his graceful body and arrogant regard.

She faced him with a bravado she was far from feeling. 'Please don't concern yourself on my part, *señor*,' she tossed her head, 'I've several options open to me. For instance, I can return to England or I can find work in Spain.' She made a nonchalant gesture with her shoulders. 'With the tourist season just started there should be plenty of work on the Costa del Sol.'

'Yes,' he agreed, 'and plenty of people looking for it. Many with more qualifications than yourself and most with the necessary work permits.'

Mortified by his quick dismissal of her employment prospects, Pavane felt her confidence dwindle, but there was more to come. Before she could even find the sharp retort she wanted, Armando twisted the knife of his disdain in the wound he had already made in her vanity.

'Besides, *señorita*, your brother-in-law, while listing the attributes you would bring to my brother as his wife, informed me that you were studying the piano and guitar at a famous London college before your aunt's death forced you to leave without qualification.' Dark brows lifted in gentle amusement. 'I imagine you

yourself would admit that in Spain of all places the
opportunities for a half-trained guitarist are hardly
numerous!'

Half-trained indeed! Even though the piano had
been her first instrument of study, she was no mean
performer on a Spanish guitar. How dared he try to
belittle her achievements! For a moment her stormy
eyes met the silent laughter of his dark gaze, before
she decided that discretion would be the better part of
valour in this abrasive confrontation. She moved her
shoulders diffidently.

'Then I'll return to England.'

'You can afford to do so?'

'I imagine Rodrigo would lend me my return fare
home. It can hardly be his ambition to see me walking
the streets of Seville, however low his opinion of me
is.'

'Nor mine either, I assure you.' His hard dark eyes
held her attention. 'I have no wish to see you hurt.'

'Oh . . .' For a moment she wondered if his attitude
towards her could be softening. Did he perhaps have a
spark of compassion under that stern formality?

As if he had guessed her thoughts and was anxious
to dispel them he added, 'Your welfare has become a
matter of family honour for me now. My name is
regarded with respect in this area and I mean to
uphold its obligations, however inconvenient.'

'Well, I don't consider myself as one of your
"family obligations"' Pavane flared back, angered by
the words. 'You can explain to Rodrigo that I'm not
good enough for your brother and suggest the best
way to get rid of such an embarrassment is to send me
back to London and forget about me!'

'Not such an easy thing to do,' Armando drawled,
taking the opportunity to run his slow gaze over her as
she sat there fuming. If the look had held admiration
she might have been ruffled, but flattered. As it was,

she fancied his glance held amusement, making her conscious of her cheap clothes and tousled hair. No wonder he didn't see her as a wife for Perico! 'And what would you do when you arrived in London?'

'Find a hostel, sign on at the job centre, apply for unemployment benefit . . .' Her voice faltered to a stop. How dismal the prospect sounded! She didn't even know if she would be entitled to unemployment benefit. The fact was she wouldn't know what to do! Still, she could find out. Other girls had to. If only the money left by her parents had been more wisely invested, but since her aunt's death it had become woefully clear there had been nothing left to help her over the difficult period between leaving college and getting employment.

She became aware of Armando regarding her with a grim smile as he saw and interpreted the flashes of emotion that coloured her expression.

'As it happens I'm able to offer you a job on a temporary basis, which will at least give you time to think about your future.'

She leaned forward eagerly. 'A job? Here on your estate, you mean?'

Before he could answer there was a light tap on the door, which opened immediately as a young woman walked into the room. She self-consciously tossed her long black hair across the shoulders of her white silk blouse as she entered, her riding boots clicking a staccato message as she walked boldly over towards Armando, who rose politely to greet her.

'What on earth are you doing here, Armando?' she pouted prettily, her dark eyes flirting with him. 'I thought you employed a manager to do all this!' Her hand gestured vaguely at the documents spread out before him.

'So I do,' he replied gravely. 'And at the moment he's sorting out some problem over at the stables.'

'I thought we might go for a ride this morning. I came over through the woods on Sultan especially.' Pavane watched as the Spanish girl smiled beguilingly. 'Will you come with me, Armando?'

'Not now, Isabella,' he shook his head, but his face was relaxed, the hard lines softened with something that could have been affection. 'As you can see,' he nodded towards Pavane, 'I'm busy.'

'Oh . . . yes.' Isabella tossed a cursory glance over her shoulder. 'Will it take long?' She placed one slim hip on the edge of the desk, resting her hand on her black-trousered thigh. 'Whatever you're doing here can't be that important!'

Only slightly chagrined at being dismissed out of hand, Pavane found herself hiding a smile. Apparently Isabella knew how to handle the formidable Spaniard. Not surprising really, because she was absolutely lovely with her dark skin and luxuriant hair. But she had misjudged Armando and realised it the instant he frowned. 'On the contrary, it's very important,' he corrected firmly. 'There's no way I shall be free to go riding with you this morning. Tomorrow—perhaps.'

He walked round the desk as she showed no intention of moving, and took her by the shoulders. She allowed him to hold her, turning in his grasp and, standing very close to him, she lifted reproachful eyes.

'Tomorrow—certainly,' she pleaded.

But he shook his head slightly, the frown deepening as he propelled her towards the door. 'I'll phone you if it's possible,' was all he would say.

'Oh, Armando!' Again the practised pout of a flirt. 'You're impossible. I don't know why I bother with you!'

'Because you want me to persuade your father you're capable of riding one of my Arab mares,' he said drily.

She laughed, but the trill of amusement didn't quite

hide the pique. 'Oh, well—get on with your business!' she told him pertly, and turning on her heel left the room, closing the door with a decided bang behind her.

Raising his eyebrows at her sudden departure, Armando turned his attention to Pavane. 'My neighbour's daughter—Isabella Cortez,' he explained laconically. 'I did leave instructions that I wasn't to be interrupted, but I'm afraid Isabella considers herself an exception to the rule.'

'She certainly seemed at home here,' Pavane agreed, a small smile curving her mouth at Armando's obvious irritation.

'She has the freedom of this house as if she were my sister,' he retorted coolly. 'However, I would require a sister to be more circumspect than to disobey my precise instructions. At times Isabella presumes on my affection too much!' He spoke the last words quietly as if to himself, but Pavane caught the inflection of annoyance and her smile deepened.

'Perhaps you indulge her too much,' she suggested softly, and was instantly rewarded by a sharp look.

'Perhaps I do,' he agreed. 'But then it's hardly your place to comment on it.'

'I'm sorry.' She flushed. For a moment she had forgotten she wasn't there to be treated as an equal, but he had spurred her response by his own reaction. 'You were talking to me about a job?' she prompted helpfully, anxious to change the subject.

He nodded, walking past her to sit down again behind the desk. 'I've another brother—Ramón.' He paused as if gathering his thoughts as she sat waiting. 'He and his wife, Dolores, are going to Brazil for three months on business and wish to leave their son in Spain. I've agreed that he can live here with me, but I won't have the time to give him the attention he needs.' He regarded her closely. 'Pablo is a bright, clever lad of nine years. He needs someone who can be responsible for his safety and pleasure.'

'You want a governess?' The idea intrigued her.

'No. There's no question of lessons. He'll be on holiday. I need someone to be a friend and companion, but someone to control him as well. This is a very large estate—over twelve thousand acres.' He gestured with his hand. 'The boundaries are over four miles square. Apart from the grain and fodder crops there are also sheep and pigs, large areas of grassland, cattle and horses. Also, of course, we have stretches of forest, notably the cork-oaks on our southern boundary.' His intent eyes regarded her unblinkingly. 'All in all it's a large and potentially dangerous place for a nine-year-old boy.'

It was an unexpected solution, but she would be stupid not to consider it. Three months, he had said. It might even be long enough time for Rodrigo's attitude to soften towards her. It would certainly give her a badly needed respite.

She could feel Armando's sardonic gaze upon her, watching and evaluating the look of relief he must have perceived on her face.

'You'd find such a job acceptable?'

Pavane glanced up at him, seeing an inexplicable cynicism in the curve of his mouth and a glimmer of self-mockery in his eyes re-awakening her earlier antagonism towards him.

'I'm surprised you consider me suitable,' she told him tartly. 'I'd have thought my reputation too badly damaged to be entrusted with the care of your nephew.'

It was a rash remark and she regretted it immediately as she saw the flash of anger in his eyes, but when he spoke again his voice was devoid of rough emotion.

'But then you see I'm a tolerant man, Pavane.'

It was such a bare-faced lie her mouth opened protestingly, but before she could utter even one word of the many that sprang to her mind. Armando continued smoothly. 'Valmontez went to great lengths to explain your background to me. He spoke highly of your family, the reputation and respect your parents earned for themselves.'

Had she imagined it or had his voice softened marginally at the mention of her dead parents? A quick glance showed what might have been compassion on that saturnine face before it was replaced by a gleam of devilment that promised her no favours. 'I can understand how difficult it must have been for an elderly lady, however well-intentioned, to bring up a young girl, to curb her headstrong behaviour and to school her in the kind of social and moral ethics a well-bred Spanish girl would be expected to learn.'

As Pavane clenched her jaw in a determined effort to bite back the angry words that would exonerate her at Melody's expense and made a silent count to ten, Armando's voice deepened with disapproval.

'You're quite right, though. As things stand at the moment you are far from a suitable candidate to whom to entrust the welfare of a young innocent boy, which is precisely the reason it will be necessary to make your standing in society beyond reproach.'

Her temper brought under control, Pavane shook her head in puzzlement. 'I don't understand.'

Armando stood up, turning his back towards her and gazing out of the window for a few moments. A slight frown creasing her forehead, Pavane stared at his broad shoulders, beneath the thin cambric shirt, admiring subconsciously the way the material narrowed to his firm waist and the taut lean line of his hips and thighs in the pale cotton trousers he was wearing. For some strange reason, she became aware her heart was tripping away at a much faster level than usual. She forced herself to breathe deeply as she watched silently while he thrust his hands into his trousers' pockets, then wheeled round to face her again.

'Naturally Ramón will wish to know who you are and how you came here. Neither would Rodrigo keep silent were you to come here merely as an employee.' He paused as if finding it difficult to determine the right words. 'Therefore, if this matter is to be resolved without loss of face for everyone concerned it will be necessary for me to marry you.'

CHAPTER FOUR

'YOU'RE joking!' It was too ludicrous to be taken seriously, and although Pavane couldn't imagine his purpose Armando was obviously playing some kind of game with her. For the first time since she had entered the room Pavane began to laugh—softly at first, then louder as the action released some of the pent-up hysteria inside her.

It was only when she saw Armando's face grow thunderously dark, his mouth tighten to a hard line, and felt a trickle of fear nudge her, that she gasped to a halt.

Staring at his furious face, she found she was clenching her hands in anxiety. She hadn't meant to offend him—but his proposal was clearly absurd.

'But that's impossible,' she blurted out. 'You can't want to marry me!'

'No,' he agreed tightly, his face still as dark as a thundercloud. 'Unfortunately, though, it appears the only solution. Valmontez has washed his hands of you. You're quite unfit to support yourself in a foreign country, and in any case should my family deny you the consideration your brother-in-law demands, this whole sordid story would soon spread. *You* may not be concerned by that fact. Accept it as a fact that *I* would. Both on my own part and on behalf of my brother.'

Pavane quailed at the icy blast of his words, resenting everything about him. Oh God, why had she got herself into this mess? But she was committed for Melody's sake. All she could do was endure it. But marriage! How could she contemplate that, with all it

48

entailed? How could she share a bed with this man
who, for all his obvious physical attractiveness, was a
stranger and one who despised her? How could she
endure his mouth on hers—his hands on her body—
the intimate act of consummation . . .

She felt the colour rise to her face as her throat
constricted. Even the thought of his body in close
contact with her own made her shiver with trepidation—and there was something else. Something that
made her first blush drain from her face leaving her
pallid and afraid. If Armando married her, the clever
web she had spun trapping herself in order to free
Melody would be torn to shreds. It would be obvious
that whomever Perico had made love to in the orange
grove, it hadn't been herself. When Armando took her
virgin body, unpractised, untaught and unwilling—he
would know the extent of her lies.

Dry-mouthed, totally unable to hide the fear on her
face as she contemplated how he would respond to
that situation, she stared back at him.

The hooded eyes that met her own were unreadable,
but when he finally spoke she realised how accurately
he had read her mind.

'Don't be alarmed, Pavane,' he said coolly. 'There is
nothing about you that would attract me to your bed.
You have the scruffy appearance of a newly-hatched
chicken, the body of a schoolgirl and the morals of a
wildcat. Hardly an irresistible formula as far as I am
concerned.'

Pavane drew her breath in with a hiss of displeasure,
her face going rigid at the spiteful words, her eyes
widening in shock at his total lack of courtesy. Here
was the bitterness and cruelty she had sensed at that
first meeting. She knew she was nothing special to
look at, but with a few phrases delivered in his deep,
cultured voice, he had stripped away what little self-
confidence still remained to her. She raised one hand

to her cheek in horror almost as if he had launched a physical attack on her. She tried to stand, but had to grab at the back of the chair when she found her legs had turned to jelly.

'Wait,' he commanded, his eyes pitiless. 'If that insults you, I make no apology. I merely wished to make my proposal clear. What I'm offering you is a marriage of expediency only.' There was a dark devil behind the glinting eyes that raked her pale face. It was as if he was determined to scratch the surface of her self-esteem. 'I happen to be selective about the women who share my bed.' His eyes travelled over her body, but she continued to face him, bravely refusing to drop her eyes. Damn his arrogance! 'When Pablo goes back to his parents and when the passage of time has smoothed these events over, the marriage can be dissolved. It will merely serve as a cover to enable you to live under this roof without drawing further scandalous gossip to your activities. It will satisfy Valmontez, restore your sister's peace of mind, release Rico from guilt and allow him to continue unhampered with his studies.' He paused, then continued. 'Ramón and Dolores will go to Brazil reassured that their son is well cared for and Pablo won't be lonely without them. As for you—it will give you time to decide where your future lies. When the marriage is ended I'll ensure that you're financially secure and happily settled in a suitable environment.'

He stopped talking, one eyebrow lifting slightly, as he awaited her answer.

There was a lot of truth in what he said, and if she had done what she had confessed to, Pavane would have felt relieved, even grateful. But there was no point in thinking along those lines. She was going to have to live out the lie for some time to come. Even so, she couldn't help the slight sulkiness edging into her voice. 'And what about you, Armando?' she challenged the glowering face. 'What advantages will you be gaining from such a grand gesture?'

He looked at her, unsmiling. 'Apart from preserving my name from unpleasant gossip, it will give me some satisfaction to see *you* leave my house having learned something of the standards of behaviour demanded from your contemporaries in this country.'

Pavane gritted her teeth. How dared he lecture her on manners!

'And *you* intend to be my tutor?' she queried, letting her mouth curl in derision, refusing to recoil from the cold look her comment earned.

'If you accept my offer, and I don't see you have any other option, then yes.' A glimmer of a smile warmed his countenance. 'Since the extent to which you will benefit when the marriage is ended will depend on the way you comport yourself, I fancy you'll make a willing pupil.'

Furious with the whole situation, unwilling to commit herself, yet seeing no easy alternative, Pavane lowered her eyes.

'There is just one question ...' It was as if Armando was deliberately keeping his voice neutral, uninvolved. 'Perico told me, under a certain amount of pressure, it's true, that he wasn't the first man you'd known: neither was there any risk of your bearing his child.'

Despite herself, Pavane gasped, raising horrified eyes to meet the intense regard of the man who had just offered her marriage. How could Perry have said such a thing about her? Her heart started hammering in protest at such an injustice and her mouth opened to refute the words, when with a sickening insight she realised that what had been said was true.

Committed as he was to upholding the lie they had both agreed on, Perry had told the truth. Whether in his heart he had been thinking of Melody or herself,

what he had said was perfectly accurate. He hadn't
seduced a virgin and neither Melody nor herself could
have conceived his child.

Armando had seen her lips move, had observed her
double-take. Now with brows furrowed, he demanded
impatiently, 'Well?'

'Does it make any difference?' she asked wearily,
unwilling to speak the words that would condemn her
utterly in his view.

'Yes, it makes a difference.' The soft-voiced reply
took her by surprise. 'In either of those circumstances
Perico would be mmade to shoulder his responsibilities.
However, I have his assurance—and whatever his sins,
Rico isn't usually a liar . . .'

'I—I . . .' she stuttered unhappily, aware that she
couldn't deny the underlying suggestion that her
acceptance of Perry's statement would imply.

He walked round the desk to place a gentle finger
beneath her small chin, persuading her to look at him.
His dark eyes burned into her and there was the first
suggestion of doubt in their depths.

'Do you want to contest what he told me, Pavane?'
he asked softly.

Close to tears, Pavane glanced desperately around
her as if seeking an answer. But she had no choice.
Miserably she returned his deep appraisal, and never
had she felt so alone in all her life.

'No,' she said stiffly. 'What he told you was the
truth. Every word.'

'It's not too late to change your mind . . .' Melody's
hands plucked distractedly at the skirt of the apple
green chiffon dress she was wearing, while her worried
eyes skimmed over the champagne satin gown that
clothed Pavane's slender body.

'Of course it's too late: much too late,' Pavane
replied calmly. 'And you know it as well as I do.'

A wicked smile curved her pale lips. 'With all the village invited, flamenco dancers hired from Seville, the kitchens laden with food, not to mention the priest all geared up for the service, however would Armando explain my not being there?'

'By admitting you were an unwilling bride in the first place,' Melody answered stonily, her sense of guilt showing in the tense expression on her face, the unhappiness of her eyes.

Pavane sat down in front of the dressing table, smoothing the satin dress carefully beneath her. The beautiful shimmering material cut with a heart-shaped neckline clung smoothly to the high, rounded curves of her breasts, fitting like a second skin to her slim waist before falling in soft folds to her ankles. The sleeves, long and traditionally narrow, completed a dress of simple perfection.

Reaching for a pale pink lipstick, Pavane met her sister's worried frown through the mirror. 'I'm not unwilling,' she said patiently. 'Neither was I forced to accept Armando's proposal. He gave me time to think about it—and I simply chose the soft option.'

'For my sake,' Melody muttered.

'For everybody's sake!' Pavane applied her lipstick carefully before continuing. 'Look, Melly, we've gone over all this a dozen times in the last fortnight. I've told you, and you alone, how hollow this marriage is going to be. What happens today is a mere façade. In fact, all I'm taking on is the job of a holiday companion to a nine-year-old boy. And there's no reason for your going about with such a long face!'

'Yes, I know.' Melody twisted her hands together. 'I know that's how you see it, and that's what's worrying me.'

Pavane ran her hand lightly over her curls, teasing

them into a soft fringe across her forehead. 'You mean you think Armando's going back on his word?' She turned to face her sister with amused eyes.

'It's a possibility I think you have to be prepared for.' The older girl's glance appraised the smiling face before her. 'You're very beautiful, you know, Pavvy, and Armando doesn't strike me as being made of wood.'

'More like steel!' Pavane agreed, then seeing the expression on her sister's face, she added briskly, 'You're talking nonsense. Me, beautiful?' Her gaze encompassed Melody's blue eyes, the sharp classic bone structure of her face, the naturally blonde hair, the slim model-like outlines of her figure. 'You're the beauty of the family, Melly. You always have been.'

Melody shook her head. 'You were always attractive, but I never realised just how lovely you were until we met again recently. Whether it was because I hadn't seen you for some time, or whether you had changed, I don't know, but you *are* beautiful: especially to a man's eyes.' Seeing Pavane's look of disbelief, she added slowly, 'Rodrigo certainly sees it. I think that was one of the reasons he was so keen to see you married. He thought your looks spelt nothing but trouble for him if you stayed under his roof unwed.'

Bemused, Pavane turned once more to the mirror, gazing at her reflection, seeing an oval face, eyes more turquoise than blue, a short straight nose, and a mouth firm and rounded above a pretty chin, all topped off by a helmet of silver blonde curls. It was the face that looked back at her every time she put her make-up on—ordinary and unremarkable to her own eyes.

'Don't worry, Melly. Armando certainly doesn't see me like that!' Odd, she thought, how the admission was painful to make.

Turning, she reached across and lifted her veil from the bed. It sprang from a tiara of cultured pearls, covering the pale curls with a milky mist. She glanced at her watch. Only another few minutes before Rodrigo would come to the door and take her down the sweeping staircase to the private chapel of the Cortijo: the chapel especially built for Armando's disfigured grandmother.

Already the guests would be in place, but it wouldn't be until after the ceremony that she would meet Ramón and Dolores and their son, who was to be her special charge.

In the days prior to the wedding she had learned a little more about Armando's family. How his father, Ignacio, had chosen to live in the Argentine until his untimely death twelve years previously. Armando had told her how he himself and his brother Ramón had returned to Spain, he to claim his heritage—the King's Farm, named after a legendary Moorish king—which had suffered under Ignacio's absentee landlordship for far too long; and Ramón to continue his career as a designer. Several years had passed before Armando's mother remarried and the seventeen-year-old Perico had beseeched his eldest brother to help him achieve his ambition of becoming a doctor.

There was no doubt that Armando had a strong sense of family loyalty, she thought with reluctant admiration. How tragic it was that Perico had behaved so irresponsibly and forced him into this bizarre situation!

Sighing deeply, she adjusted the veil. How glad she was that Rodrigo and Armando between them had taken over the planning of the wedding with the capable help of the housekeeper—a middle-aged widow named Ana who ran the Cortijo with admirable efficiency. It had come as a great relief that she wouldn't be expected to interfere in the smooth running of the established routine either then or in the future.

She had been stunned when she first realised the scale of the ceremony and celebrations which were being planned, but her tentative protest had been dismissed by Armando's curt reply. 'It will be expected of me!'

It had been his suggestion she should dress for the occasion at the Cortijo itself. Earlier that day she had brought over the suitcases containing all her worldly goods—and precious little they were, she thought wryly. When she left England she had realised it was the start of a new life for her, so apart from a basic selection of clothes, she had sold or given away her other personal effects, keeping only a few deeply cherished items—the LPs featuring her parents in concert, her favourite cassette tapes and, of course, her well loved guitar.

Her wedding dress, its accompanying veil and the beautiful champagne satin shoes, a present from Melody and Rodrigo, had all been delivered direct to the Cortijo.

'Are you all right, Pavvy?' Melody's question brought her back to the present.

'Of course,' she assured her sister. 'I'm almost ready.'

As if in direct response to her assertion there was a knock at the door and Rodrigo came in. Powerfully built and beautifully groomed, he was an imposing figure. Little wonder he had captured Melody's heart, and the affection in his gaze was clear to see as it swept over his wife before resting on Pavane.

'Everyone is in place,' he told her quietly. 'Are you ready?'

She took a deep breath. Suddenly her legs felt weak and her heart was a living thing fluttering like a bird behind the soft satin that encased her breast. How many times had she dreamed of the day she would walk down the aisle to be joined in the sight of God to the man she loved. Instead she was acting a part in a bitter travesty and the dark handsome face of the man who would turn to await her would mirror only his contempt for the woman he thought her to be.

'Yes, I'm ready.'

She laid her hand on Rodrigo's arm, immeasurably touched when he covered it with his free palm. It was a gesture that offered her forgiveness and wished her happiness. There was no need for him to put the emotions into words.

The warm perfumed air of the Spanish night caressed the wedding guests as they sat or strolled around the flower decked patio. Pavane stood in the shadows drinking in the scene, determined never to forget the magic of the night and the music.

The performance of the flamenco was nearly at an end. She like the others, had listened, watched and admired, caught up in its colourful passion.

Now, while the musicians paused, she could look back on the wedding ceremony and acknowledge to herself that it had been beautiful. She had walked into the small church to find it newly decorated and polished and simply awash with flowers, their heady perfume coming in a wave to engulf her as she had walked down the aisle to where Ramón and Armando awaited her.

Armando had turned to watch her progress, and unwittingly her hand had clutched heavily at Rodrigo's arm for support. Suddenly struck with a dreadful feeling of guilt that she was about to take meaningless vows and call upon God to witness them, she felt her eyes fill with tears of remorse, her mind sending up a desperate prayer for forgiveness.

She hadn't dared to blink or the tears would have spilled. As she reached Armando's side he had gazed down into her enormous moisture-glazed eyes and she had seen such a look of mingled hurt and despair on his serious face that she had forced her mouth into a smile, touching his arm in an instinctive gesture of comfort as a warm compassion flowed through her. The ceremony was as much an ordeal for him as it was for her, after all.

He had flinched at her touch, but afterwards she had maintained her self-control, making her vows in a quiet voice with only a hint of a tremble. Armando's responses had been low but firm and the hand that took hers had not wavered as he slid the thick gold band on her finger.

Later when his cool lips had brushed across her cheek, a strange thrill had tingled through her body, and she had wondered what it would be like to be the woman he loved.

Watching now, she saw the leader of the flamenco group resume his chair. The chattering crowd grew silent as he lifted his head and commenced the finale of the evening's entertainment. Mystical and magical, plumbing the very depths of emotion, plunging from heaven to touch the blackness of hell, the singer opened his heart. This, Pavane knew, was the Canto Jondo, the 'deep' song of flamenco which had its roots in the Church. Inexperienced as she was in the performance of the song, Pavane was too much of a musician not to be aware that the singer was enjoying a state of grace that can affect all performers at times, lifting the well-rehearsed mundane into something approaching the sublime.

There was not a sound to be heard as the song climbed to the stars, weaving a spell that touched her soul. As the last aching notes drifted into nothingness, Pavane glimpsed Melody and Rodrigo among the close circle of the audience. Even as she watched, she saw Rodrigo's hands clasped tightly on her sister's shoulders and saw the joy on Melody's face as she turned her head and smiled ecstatically into his dark, intense face.

Their happiness was a tangible presence, a visual answer to her desperate prayer. She had done the right thing. If nothing else good had come of the day, she must at least be able to take part of the credit for their reconciliation.

'Pavane! I must talk to you.'

'Oh!' She spun round at the low masculine voice and the touch of a hand on her satin-clad arm. 'Perry! You made me jump!' The coolness of her voice wasn't assumed.

'I'm sorry,' he brushed her protest aside, 'I've been trying to get you alone all afternoon. Is there anywhere we can go to talk?'

'Armando's gone in to have a word with Ana. Can't we talk here?'

'No,' he said adamantly, glancing around. 'There are too many people about. Will you come into the Cortijo with me?'

'If you insist,' she agreed reluctantly. 'But you'll have to lead the way. You know the layout better than I.'

He nodded, already guiding her towards the building. 'Follow me.'

He took her into a room on the ground floor, closing the door behind him and turning immediately to face her, his young face strained and anxious.

'Pavane, listen, you must believe me.' His dark eyes swept her face. 'When Armando packed me off to Madrid like that, I had no idea what he intended. He just told me he would sort the matter out so no one got hurt!'

'As he has done,' she retorted calmly. Perico didn't deserve pity, but his conscience was obviously giving him a bad time.

'You haven't been forced into this?' His penetrating gaze asked for the truth.

She shook her head. 'Of course not.'

She heard him sigh with deep relief. 'Thank God!' His face relaxed into a grin. 'You certainly made an outstanding couple. Now I know you really care for each other, I can offer my congratulations without feeling a louse.'

'Thank you.' Pavane accepted his words graciously, aware Armando hadn't told him how spurious their relationship was to be.

Perico took a step nearer to her, putting out his hands and taking her by the shoulders, holding her with a firmness which betrayed his agitation. 'I've been speaking to Melody. She told me what Rodrigo was going to do to me—what your intervention saved me from. Oh God . . .' His voice broke. 'It's a debt I'm never going to be able to repay.'

The agony on his proud young face was so marked, even the thought of Rodrigo's intended vengeance so obviously horrific to him, that Pavane made no attempt to free herself from his grip. 'But if there's anything I can ever do for you, at any time, for any reason, let me know.' To her surprise he leant forward and pressed his cheek against hers in an impulsive gesture of gratitude.

The next instant the door behind them swung open with violence and Armando strode into the room as Perico, reacting with quicksilver reflexes, pushed her away from him, his face flushing with embarrassment.

Pavane said nothing, feeling an indefinable weakness spread through her limbs as she gazed at her husband's dark face, closed and unfathomable. She could feel his keen, penetrating eyes burning into her. Automatically she raised her hand to her throat as if she were in danger of suffocating. For several seconds his gaze held hers unwaveringly as she found herself unable to break the invisible beam that seared into her mind.

'Sit down, Rico.' Armando's voice, soft and smooth as clotted cream addressed his brother, but the impaling power of his accusing eyes was all for her.

Slowly and deliberately he looked her over, his head a little to one side as if he was studying a bargain, his imagination watching her flesh cringe beneath the virginal purity of the dress she wore. Beneath that impertinent scrutiny she was silent, guessing his thoughts: unable to justify herself.

Perico, pale now with tiny beads of sweat clinging to his forehead, cleared his throat as if to speak, then apparently thinking better of it, did as he was bid, subsiding on one of the chairs.

'Armando . . .' His name came out as a croak from Pavane's parched lips as she tried to free herself from the contempt which glazed his expression.

'Later, *amada* . . . later.'

A quiver of apprehension raced through her, as she recognised a threat in the gentle words: a terrible irony in the endearment.

She hesitated, her fingers nervously smoothing the oyster perfection of her skirt. 'Armando, please . . . I . . .'

'Later,' he repeated. Never had she seen such bitterness on anyone's face, or searched more helplessly for words to dispel it. 'I need to speak to my brother alone.'

To defy him could only make matters worse, yet still she found herself unable to walk away.

'It's very late, *esposa mia*, and it's been a tiring day for you. Most of our guests are leaving and they will hardly expect to see you still up at this hour. They will imagine you already preparing yourself for the joys of the night which traditionally follow the joys of the wedding day, no?'

The mocking words broke the spell that had transfixed her as he added, 'Go up to your room,

Pavane. I'll see you later.'

With one last worried glance at Perico, who was sitting with his head supported by his hands, Pavane moved obediently towards the door, conscious that Armando's words had brought a sudden flush of scarlet to her pale face.

CHAPTER FIVE

ALONE in the room where she had put on her wedding dress, Pavane now disrobed, hung the lovely garment in the large built-in wardrobe which ran one length of the wall. Certainly the Cortijo had been well modernised: but then it appeared that anything Armando undertook was always effected to his satisfaction.

Reluctantly she surveyed the remainder of her clothes, admitting to herself how inadequate they were. Although Aunt Elaine had been generosity itself where the majority of things were concerned, clothes had been her one blind spot, and Pavane's limited wardrobe reflected her influence.

With a sigh she slid the doors of the wardrobe shut, turning towards the bed which had been turned down, smiling at the sight of her shortie nylon nightdress draped across the pillow.

Slithering her full-length slip over her hips, she wondered what the maids had thought when they saw she and Armando were having separate rooms. With a communicating door, it was true . . . Her glance moved across to that very door, eyeing it with some disquiet. What had he meant when he said he would see her later? Did he mean that night or the following day? Surely it was too late for any discussion now. He must have meant tomorrow.

Quickly she stripped off the remainder of her clothes and pulled the nightdress over her head. All she wanted to do was wash her tired face and brush her teeth. It would be time enough to cope with tomorrow when it came!

Perhaps it was the sound of the running water which lulled her senses, but she didn't hear the bedroom door open. Emerging from the bathroom, her hand running wearily through her curls, she came to a sudden shocked standstill on finding herself face to face with her newly-acquired husband.

Armando sat negligently on the side of the bed, one dark trousered leg resting on the thigh of the other. His white wedding shirt was tieless, the first couple of buttons undone to reveal the firm line of his throat. He, too, looked tired, but the darkness under his eyes added quality to his appearance, as did the heaviness of his eyelids with their fringe of sable lashes, adding a magnetic essence to a face that was already prepossessing.

Pavane uttered a little cry of surprise, instantly aware of her state of undress and the length of shapely leg on show beneath the mid-thigh frill that brushed against her.

Armando raised a lazy eyebrow at her expression. 'I told you I'd see you later.' There was a lurking air of amusement about his attitude which only served to confuse her further.

'Yes, I know. I didn't hear you come in.' Furtively she glanced around. Was there anything within reach which she could drape over her shoulders to hide the rounded curves of her body so obviously displayed through the filmy material? She had no wrap with her, having left her old candlewick dressing-gown in England—it was hardly the thing for southern Spain! Could she take refuge in the bed? No, she couldn't. Not with Armando sitting there, his vibrant masculinity dominating the room, his gaze lingering with interest on her state of undress. Suddenly the bed was the last place she wanted to be!

Her anxious glance revealing nothing that would add to her modesty, she walked rather desperately across the room to a large armchair, curling herself into its depths and drawing her legs beneath her, conscious all the time of the sardonic glimmer of her husband's eyes.

'Isn't it rather late to portray such an air of chastity?' he asked drily. 'Or am I being made an exception to the men who have enjoyed the sight of your underclad body?'

There was an undercurrent of reproach in the question that stung her. Angry eyes emphasised her reaction. 'If you mean is it my intention to behave like a normal wife, then the answer is "no, of course it isn't,"' she replied with spirit. 'You made it quite clear that my job here is companion to your nephew, and I've no wish to prejudice that.'

'Ah, yes.' He met her antagonistic gaze with piercing appraisal. 'That's one of the things I want to speak to you about. That little episode with Perico this evening won't be repeated.'

'That's an order, is it?' She was being stupid to challenge him. It wasn't his fault he had such a poor opinion of her and she would have to learn to bear with it, but no man had ever looked at her with such a mixture of scorn and disapproval, or attempted to force his will on her.

She had believed once he'd gone through the motions of saving his cherished 'honour', he would ignore her. Now for the first time she had doubts. The studied coolness with which he regarded her did nothing to quell the rising pangs of fear that had quickened her heartbeat.

'It's a statement of fact. I've told him he's no longer welcome here.'

'Oh, but that's desperately unfair!' Unthinkingly she flew to Perry's defence. 'This is his home!'

'On the contrary, it's *my* home,' Armando corrected gravely. 'And therefore it's *my* decision as to whom I share it with.' He stared at her unblinking, mesmer- ising her by the power in his dark eyes. 'Large though it is, it's not big enough to hold you and my brother at the same time.' He paused long enough to let the words sink in. 'As you both demonstrated this afternoon.'

'I think you're misjudging the importance of what you saw.' Pavane's fingers intertwined with nervous- ness. 'Perry was naturally rather shocked at your sudden decision to marry and in such—such . . .' Conscious of his unwavering gaze, she sought for a word that wouldn't offend him or condemn herself. 'In such unusual circumstances,' she finished weakly. 'He wanted to make sure I hadn't been forced into anything against my will.'

'And what did he propose to do about it if you had?' For a moment amusement glittered on his lean face. 'Challenge me to a duel?'

She shrugged her shoulders, unnerved by his reaction. 'He was just uncertain and feeling guilty. I suppose he wanted absolution.'

'Which you gave him, no doubt. The kiss of pardon, I believe it's called.'

Oh, why on earth couldn't he let the matter rest! Still, she admitted, it must have looked bad from his point of view—seeing her in the arms of the man he believed to have been her lover.

'I told him I married you because I wanted to. The kiss he gave me was just a brotherly embrace to wish me happiness,' she told him firmly, watching his face.

The trouble was, he was so much of a stranger to her it was difficult to judge his emotions. If he was angry, his temper was certainly under control. Yet she wasn't so naïve as to believe he was regarding her with anything like approval. There was an air about him she found frankly disturbing. Something about his lazy appraisal of her that made her achingly aware of his arrant masculinity. Remembering Melody's reservations about the terms of the marriage she had entered into, Pavane felt a cold shiver tremble through her body.

'Good!' But there was no smile on his face to echo the word. 'Then you won't feel too deprived by his absence. But there is something I have to make quite clear to you, *querida*.' The endearment was a soft growl in his throat. A verbal caress spoken with a cynicism that couldn't entirely destroy the beauty of its sound. 'While you're masquerading as my wife, you'll treat both me and my standing as your husband with respect!' His stubborn chin lifted autocratically, much in the manner of a matador when he challenges the bull to attack him.

'Naturally your pride must be maintained,' she agreed tartly, nettled by the implied reprimand. 'I imagine the impressive ceremony we've just been through had that as its aim as well!'

Armando's face stilled, but his body which had been lounging easily on the bed tautened as he swung round to sit gazing at her intently.

Pavane felt her pulse quicken alarmingly, wondering what emotions lay behind the glittering darkness of those eyes. There was something about his attitude that made her want to flaunt her vulnerability, to test the limits of his endurance.

She controlled the tremor in her voice. 'Perhaps playing the *patrón* so regally ensures the loyalty of your workers?' she suggested with a questioning lift of one eyebrow. 'Does laying on a feast and musicians help to keep the wages bill low?'

'You're scarcely in a position to criticise the way I run my life or question my motives.' There was ice in Armando's voice. Unwillingly she shivered, feeling goose pimples of apprehension gather on her exposed skin. The glance he had shot her was scathing.

Whether she liked it or not, by marrying Perico's brother she had placed herself under his jurisdiction, totally within his power, and she had little doubt he intended to exercise every bit of authority both law and custom gave him.

She stayed silent, subdued by the edge of anger that had sharpened his tone. After a short pause he spoke again.

'You have a lot to learn about the way we live here, Pavane. By the time you leave I intend you shall be a lot wiser than you are now.'

'An expert on agricultural management?' she asked innocently, deliberately ignoring the disguised threat in his promise.

She was totally unprepared for the quality of the smile that transformed his face. 'That too,' he agreed. 'Although unless you particularly want a lesson on agricultural methods at this moment, I shall let my manager, Enrico, explain our policies to you when he gives you a guided tour of the estate tomorrow.'

There was a devilish gleam in his frankly sensuous eyes as they caressed her with unexpected humour. 'This I will tell you, though. In Andalusia there are two kinds of farms—the large ones like this covering over six hundred and fifty acres, which are known as *latiofundios*, and the *minifundios*, tiny plots of land divided and subdivided over the years so that over thirty-five million of them are less than two-and-a-half acres each.'

Pavane raised her eyes and nodded attentively. It seemed she was going to get a lecture on agricultural methods after all! Having caught his gaze, she hesitated, seeing something she couldn't quite define lurking behind his shadowed eyes. His words unnerved her still further. 'In many ways the lesson we've learned from farming can be applied to women,' he continued. 'The plots that are divided and owned by many different people never achieve their true potential. It is the *latiofundio*, owned and cultivated by one master, which fulfils its promise and gives the greatest yield.'

Lazily he got to his feet, walking round the bed towards her. 'It's the same with a woman, *dulzura mia*. If she spreads her favours too freely she will always lack fulfilment.'

'How very profound!' Pavane stared back at him, aware that her heart was beating erratically, but totally unaware of her darkened pupils and trembling mouth, as something within her responded to the hidden vibrations that emanated from Armando's hard, lean body.

She'd wanted to be indifferent to him, but there was a quality in him which she couldn't define. Whatever it was, it had shattered that indifference, seized her antagonism and begun to mould it into something quite different. She daren't question too closely the tingling warmth that pervaded her body as he approached her, for the answer might be too disturbing for her continued peace of mind.

Pulling herself together with an effort, she raised amused eyes. 'Presumably your theory also applies to men?' she questioned facetiously. Watching him through quickly lowered lashes she saw the gleam of laughter sparkle in his eyes.

'Not in quite the same way. Man is after all the farmer in this sense. He is the active one whose dream is for a plot of virgin soil that will repay his attention a hundredfold, is he not? If he finds a piece of land that's open to cultivation, why shouldn't he sample it—then abandon it if it displeases him?'

Pavane stirred helplessly as he sat down on the arm of her chair, lounging with a supple male grace, one arm resting across its back.

Uncertain as to whether he was taunting her or

flirting with her, she only knew she was being led into a conversation that had nothing at all to do with farming, and she was very doubtful as to the wisdom of continuing it!

'I—I'm not very versed in farming,' she muttered at length, feeling something was expected of her and angry to find she was trembling.

Armando was watching her carefully, his face still bearing a slight smile. 'Neither, *amada*, are you as unwilling to share my bed as you would have me believe.'

The words were so softly spoken it took her a moment to realise what he had said. When his hand dropped with a soft movement to her shoulder she was left in no doubt. Instantly she uncurled her body, rising to her feet in an attempt to escape his embrace. Senses leaping, heart racing in a mixture of expectation and trepidation, she was forced to acknowledge that the awareness flaring between them was glowing with a brilliance that was as dangerously exciting as it was unwelcome.

Confused and unsure, she backed away from his threatening presence. Surely he didn't mean to touch her? Fighting her rising panic, she told herself he must be teasing her for his own amusement or, worse still, conducting some cold-blooded experiment to see how easy she would be to seduce, before humiliating her by rejecting her. Yet cold-blooded wasn't an epithet she could apply to Armando at that instant. The smile that turned the corners of his strong mouth and softened the lustrous depths of his dark eyes would be more likely to set a fire raging in a woman's body than to start a second ice-age!

'Pavane . . .' He had risen with her, moved in front of her, one arm came to encircle her body just above the waist. The other hand moved to rest beneath her chin, forcing her to meet his eyes. In desperation she tried to turn away from him, not caring for the soft drawl with which he had spoken her name. But he held her firmly, midnight eyes mocking her. 'Do you find me so repulsive then, *chica*?'

She found him many things, but never that, and it was clear he knew it. Now particularly the firmness of his arm round her slender body was warm and welcoming, the strong elegant fingers beneath her chin disturbing, but not cruel. She was so close to him she was being overpowered by a force totally beyond her comprehension.

How could she admit to him how his nearness was making her legs turn to jelly? How could she explain the strange yearning that shivered through her body when she didn't even fully understand it herself? But she must answer him!

'I don't really know you.' Her agitation made her voice shake.

'You've known me as long as you knew my brother.' The arm round her tightened, pulling her closer towards him so that she gasped in shock at the sudden contact of their bodies. 'But don't worry, I'm not as greedy as Perico.' He laughed, a low cynical burr of amusement. 'I only want to test the soil for acidity—not plant the crop!'

For an instant as he lowered his head towards her, his purpose clear, Pavane resolved to resist the kiss he intended to plant on her pale mouth. With a single moan of rejection she raised her hands to push against his chest in an idle attempt to keep him at bay.

She had anticipated a brutal assault, a salutary lesson to impress his contempt. Dear God, how she had misjudged him! The slightly parted lips that touched and teased her firmly clamped mouth were gentle harbingers of pleasure. Relief at his gentleness drained her body of tension. When the tip of his tongue followed the outline of her lips, tickling the delicate skin, she parted them, her resistance to his caresses stillborn.

She hadn't anticipated the strength of her own reactions beneath the insistent pressure of his hard, silky mouth. She hadn't known that her breasts would tingle as if an electric current had charged them, or that such a sensation of warm weakness would flood through her body. Nothing like this had happened when Kevin had kissed her. Then she had felt unmoved, even faintly embarrassed, uncomfortable, as their features had moved awkwardly against each other's.

There was nothing awkward about Armando. From the warm erotic fragrance of his skin and hair, the subtle indescribable flavour of his mouth, the hint of a quiver she sensed behind the muscle-hardened flesh of his ardent body, to the slow hypnotic movement of his hand against her spine, Armando's actions showed a wicked expertise that must have come from experience as well as innate passion.

Nothing of this mattered as, caught in forces beyond her understanding or control, Pavane slid her arms round his firm body, feeling the smooth, rounded muscles of his shoulders beneath the fine wedding shirt. Shutting her eyes in silent ecstasy, with her hands she told him of her pleasure, reaching for the proud column of his neck, venturing with trembling finger tips through the silky hair.

As his mouth pleasured her, possessing it with total mastery, she pressed herself in unconscious abandonment against his resilient body, increasing her own tension as her breasts rubbed against his chest.

She felt his hand drift away from her back, then his fingers touch the hem of her nightdress. Her body stiffened in instant rejection as his palm moved on bare flesh, flinching with shock as it travelled a smooth path over the curve of her hips. With her mouth sealed by his own, she was unable to cry out her protest, but he must have felt her withdrawal! Forced to cling to him to prevent herself from overbalancing, she felt the growing extent of his arousal and began to panic, her fingers digging into his flesh in wordless protest.

She was shaking when Armando finally released her mouth with a shuddering sigh, his breathing harsh and laboured, his hand still encircling her body beneath the flimsy covering.

'Please, Armando ...' she begged tremulously, 'I didn't mean ... I didn't want ...'

'What didn't you want, *amada*?' A sardonic humour gleamed in his lustrous eyes as he breathed the question against the soft skin of her cheek.

Ashamed at the lack of control she had shown, Pavane dropped her gaze beneath his knowing look. Excitement had flowed through her like a tidal wave, washing away her natural caution, making her totally unaware of what she was doing. She had succumbed to a subtle magic spun by the man who was her husband, yet who had vowed not to exercise his physical rights. She had felt safe to experiment, to indulge her newly discovered reactions at his expense.

Looking at his expression, seeing the rapid pulse at his throat, the flush across his high cheekbones, she was regretting her behaviour. 'I didn't want you to— to make love to me!'

'You mean you prefer Perico as a lover?' The words were cruel, but the hand that ruffled her soft curls was gentle. 'But then I've only just completed a little preliminary research, *amada mia*. You mustn't judge me on a simple kiss!'

A simple kiss! If that was simple what was complex? 'You're deliberately misunderstanding me,' she whispered, painfully aware of the warm throbbing of her mouth, 'All I want to do is go to bed.'

'And so you shall, *querida*!'

Before she realised his intention he swung her off her feet, striding over to the bed, laying her down upon it and following her in one easy, graceful movement.

Embarrassed, yet strangely excited, she tried to roll away from his confining body as the nightdress slid upwards. She was no match for him as, ignoring her struggles, he seized possession of her lips yet again, his hand finding the erect peaks of her breasts, teasing and touching their dark-hued beauty, bringing them to an aching prominence before taking their throbbing stiffness into the sweet sanctuary of his mouth.

She was lost in sensation so totally alien, so utterly exquisite, all thought of fighting him left her as she pressed her head back into the pillow, arching her back in unwitting surrender.

'Now . . .' The word slid from his slightly parted lips. Looking at the glazed surface of his slumbrous eyes, the tautness of the skin across his cheekbones, the deepening shadows beneath his eyes, Pavane wondered how long he could continue to administer this sweet torment to her when he had no intention of taking it to a natural conclusion.

'Now . . .' he said again, softly, 'give me your hand, Pavane: let me feel it on my face. Touch me as if you wanted me to be your lover . . .'

Wonderingly, she did as he bade her, her sensitive fingers feeling the incipient thrust of dark beard beneath the polished silk of his skin. She explored the contours of his face, her thumb brushing the thick dark eyebrows, touching the brush of black lashes, moving downwards to his mouth with its long curved bow with its promise of strength and sensuality.

He was lying above her, but slightly to one side, bearing his own weight, as his right hand lingered in the hollow of her waist.

'Come on, my darling,' he urged her, his voice vibrant and husky. 'You have no need to play the virgin. Undo my shirt, let me feel your cool hands against my heart.'

Blindly she obeyed, compelled as much by her own instincts as by his command. She reached across, easing the small buttons through their holes, pushing the cloth aside, her attention transfixed by the sight of his naked chest deeply tanned, the muscles smooth and rippling.

'That's better ...' The words escaped as a sigh as he pushed her back into the pillows, moving across her so their bare flesh touched.

Dream or nightmare? In her bemused state Pavane couldn't rationalise. A violent instinctive chemistry or the beginning of a miracle? All she knew for a fact was that her mind and body were singing in unison and her loins were beginning to tremble with the rhythm of love. So this was what it was like to want a man. In her wildest dreams she could never have imagined how it would feel.

As Armando's hand moved erotically down from her waist, stroking the sensitive curve of her abdomen, edging towards the centre of her own deep arousal, she forgot everything except the magic of his touch; forgot his avowal; forgot that if he did make love to her, her masquerade would be completely revealed; forgot what that revelation would do to Melody's life and Perry's and her own ...

Shuddering in deep ecstasy, enfolding his vibrant male body in her arms, accepting the intimate caresses with joy and abandonment, she put the flood of warm feeling that enveloped her into the only words she could. '*Querido, mi querido* ... I love you ... I love you!'

As if the words had broken the spell, destroyed the current that charged them both with shared emotion,

Armando's body grew still above her. Scarcely daring to breathe, she felt him roll away from her. She stared in aching disbelief as he smoothed the folds of her nightdress over her body, watched with a growing dread his face grow cold and expressionless.

'Love?' The word scorched her as if it had been a brand. 'Love is a myth—the fancy dress worn by desire—discarded when it has been satisfied.'

'You're a cynic!' she accused breathlessly, her romantic ideals toppled before the blast of his scorn, her body bereft and abandoned by his sudden withdrawal.

'A realist!' Armando retorted bitterly.

He was pulling the edges of his shirt together, threading the buttons through the buttonholes. Her fantasy shattered, it gave Pavane some satisfaction to see how badly his fingers shook.

'My God, Pavane! If Rico had "loved" you, do you really suppose he would have stood aside and let me marry you?'

'I know he never loved me . . .' She had spoken before realising how the unthinking admission would blacken her.

As his dark Latin eyes raked the soft outlines of her body with an insulting appraisal she clutched at the crumpled bed cover, raising it to her neck.

Armando bared his teeth in the semblance of a smile. 'Relax, *mi amor*. I have more discretion than my brother. I have no taste to play understudy to Rico.'

Oh, how dared he speak to her like that! She drew her breath in with an audible hiss. Who had started the whole thing anyway? If it had been his intention to insult and humiliate her, he had certainly succeeded, but she wouldn't let him escape without a dent to his ego.

'Which is just as well, because your performance lacks his integrity and polish!' she flashed back at him.

As if he hadn't heard her, Armando strode to the door between the two rooms, and without a second look at her pulled it open with venomous power, crossing the threshold and banging it behind him with barely controlled strength.

And to think in that marvellous moment she had really believed what she had cried out to him! Never, never in her life would she say those words to him again—even if he lay at her feet and begged her to. Not that there was any chance of that!

'Do you accept hate as a genuine emotion, then?' she called out at the blank face of the door in a childish attempt to vent her anger and frustration. 'Because that's what I really feel for you, Armando! I hate you!'

Then she turned on her side, switched out the bedside light, and burst into tears.

CHAPTER SIX

SUN was already filtering through the slatted blinds of her window when Pavane awakened the following morning. She had anticipated lying awake in the hours of darkness, tossing and turning as she worried about her plight, but the traumatic events of her wedding day had taken their toll and to her surprise she had slept deeply.

How she loved the early morning in Spain when the sun's heat was a gently caressing balm, when the day simmered with the promise of untold delights, when the air, scented and still, stirred the senses.

She slid out of bed, padded over to the window in bare feet, threw the blinds aside, revealed the open window and drew in great lungfuls of the sparkling air.

The first problem of the day was how on earth was she going to face Armando after last night? What had possessed her to accept his caresses? To accept and enjoy them, she corrected herself silently. She had allowed herself to be caught up in a schoolgirlish fantasy engendered by her childish dreams of marriage and encouraged by the high drama of the flamenco and the stage setting of Armando's beautiful home. What had been his real motives anyway?

Deep in thought, she walked to the bathroom, brushed her teeth and showered. Returning, she sat down on the bed, still in her nightdress, curling her legs beneath her. She had told Armando she loved him. A man who was a stranger to her, whom she only knew by reputation—and what a reputation! Morally unassailable perhaps, but cold and calculating, determined to use the power of his inherited wealth to have

his own way. She shivered spontaneously, remembering the proud hard lines of his face, speaking
of a bloodline with its pagan roots in Araby.

Such a man was outside her experience, but she
knew he bore the stamp of a race fused in a crucible
where grace and wit and suppleness of mind were the
obverse side of unbending pride, foolhardy courage
and a deep, uncompromising regard to the ideal of
honour. And she had dared to tell him she loved him!
But in that moment, with his arms about her, she had
fallen under his spell and believed it to be the truth. If
he had wanted to consummate their marriage she
would have been a willing partner, and to her eternal
shame, she had left him in no doubt of that fact.

In the clear light of day she had to find the courage
to face him, to take the part he wished her to play as if
nothing had happened between them. Probably, she
comforted herself, when she saw him again, with the
false magic of the previous night dispelled, she would
wonder what on earth she had found so irresistible
about him.

A sharp knock on the door between their rooms
interrupted her thoughts, and she swallowed nervously, determined to control the tone of her voice.
Pulling the white sheet over her legs, she called out,
'Yes?'

Armando walked into the room with a lazy smile on
his face as he met her enquiring eyes. Pavane had
expected scorn, anger, indifference, but all she could
read on that vitally attractive face was an amused
awareness.

'Ah, you're awake—good!' His keen eyes had taken
in the unshuttered window and the lack of sleepiness
on her face.

Pavane's gaze followed him as he moved further into
the room, walking towards the window to rest his
hands on the narrow sill as he gazed down at the patio.

It was clear he had been up for some time and was dressed for a semi-formal occasion. The cream coloured shirt moulded to the strong lines of his shoulders and back, the pale fawn trousers closely tailored to the lean length of thigh and calf emphasised his height with their knife-edged creases.

Pavane let her glance travel upwards towards the black hair that glistened like sable satin, her lips parting in a smile at the way the still damp tendrils were beginning to curl against the nape of his neck. They at least weren't to be cowed by his severity.

Armando turned abruptly, catching the glimmer of a smile still on her face, his level brows arching slightly as if to question the cause. Hastily she looked away.

'I have to go to Cordoba today.' He spoke without emotion. 'I can arrange for breakfast to be sent to you here, if you like.' There was only polite enquiry in the depth of the eyes that regarded her.

'I—I don't know,' she wavered, uncertain of herself in this strange environment. 'What's the general routine of the house?'

He shrugged lean shoulders. 'Breakfast is only a light meal, easily prepared and readily available. In the summer I like to eat outdoors on the patio. If you care to do the same I suggest you phone down to the kitchen and tell Ana that you'll be down shortly and let her know what you want.'

'I'll do that,' she decided verbally. 'Perhaps Pablo will join me?'

'You'll find he's already eaten this morning, but he's been told to stay on the patio till you join him.' He paused. 'I thought you should become acquainted with the Cortijo as soon as possible, so I've asked Enrico to act as guide to you this morning and take you round the estate. Pablo as well. He knows his way around, but it's too dangerous a place for a child to explore without supervision.'

'Yes, of course. You can rest assured I won't let him come to any harm.' Pavane shifted slightly, easing her position on the bed. 'I only met him yesterday, but he seems to be a very pleasant friendly child . . .'

Her statement concealed a question which Armando answered readily enough.

'Pablo won't give you any trouble. He is, as you say, well-mannered and obedient. At the same time,' he flicked her a mocking smile, 'he has the adventurous spirit and strong will of any normal boy his age, and although he won't show it, he won't take too kindly to being ordered around by a member of the "weaker" sex. So play your hand with discretion, my love, because although he is answerable to you—you are going to be answerable to me!'

'I'm well aware of my responsibilities,' she retorted frostily. 'And I hadn't seen them in the light of ordering anyone around. I'd rather hoped,' she added wistfully, 'Pablo and I could become friends.'

'I'm sure you can,' Armando accorded. Did she imagine the supercilious curl of his shapely upper lip? 'You obviously have a winning way with young men.'

'Whereas my success with older ones leaves much to be desired,' she flung back sharply. 'But I'm working on it . . .'

'Yes.' The monosyllable condemned her more than her own words and she cursed herself inwardly. Why on earth did she feel this need to provoke him, to taunt him with her own presumed frailties?

Quickly she changed the subject, feeling the unwanted blood rising to her cheeks at the echo of disgust in his reply. 'What do I do about lunch for Pablo and myself?' she asked demurely.

'Again, that's up to you. If you want anything special, please let Ana know before you go out. Otherwise there are always cold meats, cheese and salad available. Plenty of fruit, naturally.' Armando regarded her with a level stare and she wished she could pierce the coolness of that dark, enigmatic gaze. 'You'll find that I'm seldom here for lunch. I like to see what's happening round the estate, but dinner is served at eight-thirty every evening. I've told Ana to continue the routine as before.' His cool regard washed over her. 'If you wish to suggest a menu by all means consult with Ana. She knows my tastes. If there's anything else that demands your attention, I prefer you to discuss it with me first.'

'Yes, of course.' Pavane nodded her head. 'I've no wish to disrupt the smooth running of your household.' She was amazed he would even consider her approaching him with regard to domestic matters. Still, the servants were meant to presume the marriage was normal, so she must at least appear to take an interest.

'It's enough for you to disrupt my life, hmm?'

Startled by the unexpectedness of the question and the silky warmth of his tone, Pavane raised wide eyes to his quizzical expression, her heart tripping a fast light rhythm at the bright intensity of the brilliant eyes that gleamed an indecipherable message. Never in her life had she been subjected to such an appraisal. It was impossible to say what lay behind those midnight-dark eyes.

A surge of uncontrollable emotion ran riot through her body as she returned his stare. She'd been wrong to suppose he would be less attractive when she saw him again.

She knew she was breathing faster, the rise and fall of her breasts betraying her agitation under his studied scrutiny. She felt her lips part slightly from the shock of her own physical reaction. Armando caught their movement, drifting his gaze to settle on her soft trembling mouth.

When he moved towards her, it was already too late

for evasive action. His hand trapped her chin, tilting her face upwards so he could study it. Now her gaze was transfixed on his mouth—a soft, sensuous oasis set in the hard-boned desert of his face. Centred between the straight arrogant nose with its finely flared nostrils, the squared chin with its whisper of a cleft, the strong jaw and elegant cheekbones, his mouth had been designed by a master artist: the top lip a slender bow of balancing curves, the lower full and sensuous, slightly squared at the centre. A mouth meant for pleasure: to kiss and be kissed . . .

Pavane closed her eyes, felt his weight on the bed beside her, allowed his demanding hand to turn her head then his warm lips touched hers with a slow indolent pressure that killed resistance before it was born. His hand left her chin, his arm circled her shoulders, drawing her closer so she could feel the warmth of his body against her own. Her fingers went out to his shoulders as blindly she enjoyed his mouth, running her tongue over its long slow curve, mindlessly allowing him to take his pleasure at will.

It had happened so unexpectedly, she hadn't been prepared! Now, feeling her own breasts tingling with longing as they were pressed hard against Armando's chest, she sensed the hammering of his own heart, as he took sweet liberties with her own responsive mouth. Aware that she was undergoing a total physical assault on her senses, that she was responding automatically to the sight of his attractive face, the lazy touch of his lips, the soft sounds of satisfaction that burred animal-like in his throat, the warm nameless taste of him, as indescribable but as refreshing as water itself, and the subtle aroma of his skin—a mixture of soap and astringent and the erotic scent signals of a virile adult male . . . Pavane knew she would have to break his embrace.

Bringing her hands to his chest, she tried to push

him away, at the same time using all her willpower to repel him from the delights of her mouth. When at last he lifted his head she heard herself give a little gasp of relief, feeling a twinge of apprehension when she saw his brilliant, narrowed eyes and heard his rapid breathing.

'Don't look so devastated!' His beautiful mouth curled in derision as he towered above her. 'It's quite normal for a husband and wife to exchange a good-morning kiss.'

'But—but we're not properly married,' she protested, agonisingly aware of the effect his nearness was still having on her and infuriated by his seeming indifference to her feelings.

'Oh, but we are, *querida*.' There was laughter in the husky tones of his deep voice. 'In the sight of God, and the villagers of Campos Altos—not to mention my little brother Rico—we are *very* properly married!'

'You know what I mean,' Pavane muttered, dismayed and ashamed at her inexplicable response. Torn between trying to understand her own reactions and Armando's motives in tormenting her in this fashion, she raised the knuckles of her hand to her pulsating mouth.

'And I hope you know what *I* mean!' His tone had sharpened. 'We're married until the day I decide I want it otherwise!' He gave an odd little laugh. 'What's the matter, Pavane? Are you afraid I'll go too far?'

Blushing, she turned her head away from his amused glance. He was making fun of her, not guessing how limited her experience was. Limited? She could have wept. Non-existent was the word.

'Don't worry.' Armando's tone had hardened at her silence. 'I want this marriage as little as you do. But, if it ever becomes necessary to remind you that I *am* your husband, I shall do so, without compunction, in any way that pleases me!'

He turned away, hands smoothing down the crisp cotton of his shirt, his lazy stride eating up the distance to the doorway. Hand on the knob, he paused, the mocking inflection of his voice finding an echo in the velvet depths of his eyes.

'Enjoy your day, my love. I'll see you at dinner.'

Regaining her breath with difficulty, Pavane sprang to her feet as the door closed behind him. He was playing with her, teasing her as if she were some silly courtesan he'd picked up off the street. Something to laugh at, to amuse himself with up to a point, but for whom he felt nothing but a deep, bitter contempt. And that, she reminded herself stoically, was exactly what he did feel, and there wasn't much she could do about it. She didn't care to think too closely about what his final threat implied. Wasn't it enough that she had agreed to accept his authority as employer without his trying to play the heavy-handed husband, which in all honour he had no claim to be?

'Armando de Montilla y Cabra!' she spoke his name with studied venom to the blank face of the door. 'You are a brute! Cold, unfeeling and cruel!' She sucked in her breath, liking the sound of the word. '*Bruto!*' she repeated with feeling, shivering as the harsh word echoed off the unresponsive oak. Then a small smile curved her bruised lips. It would appear that if nothing else came from this doomed relationship, she would become adept at conversing with doors!

Enrico arrived in the jeep at ten o'clock, interrupting a discussion on sport between herself and Pablo which had been straining Pavane to the limits of her knowledge.

'*Buenos dias, señora.*' Enrico's smile was warm and friendly. She had met him several times since her first visit to the Cortijo and had taken an immediate liking to the sturdy middle-aged man who nominally

managed the large estate. 'I forgot to ask Armando if
you rode, so I brought the jeep for our tour—I hope
that suits you?'

'It's perfect,' she concurred. 'As a matter of fact I do
ride, but I haven't done so for some time and I
certainly don't fancy my chances on one of the Arab
stallions my—my husband breeds!'

Strange how difficult it was to say the words 'my
husband'. She cast her eyes down, hoping Enrico
hadn't noticed her embarrassment.

'Then, if you like, on our way back we'll call in at
the stables and saddle up a mare for you to complete
the tour?'

'Yes, why not?' Pavane allowed herself to be helped
into the jeep.

As they left the precincts of the house to travel
alongside the vast fields already showing the promise
of a good harvest, Pavane gazed at the impressive
spread in amazement. She had never seen farming on
such a grand scale before. Armando had already told
her that apart from grain and fodder they also engaged
in animal husbandry. Such wide diversification
fascinated her.

'How long has my husband been breeding horses?'
she asked.

'Armando's Arabs?' Enrico grinned, his weather-
beaten face showing laughter lines. 'About four
years now. A recent undertaking and like everything
else he's done over the past decade, promising to be
very successful. We have clients from riding schools
all over Spain.'

'Have you always worked at the Cortijo?' she asked
with deep interest.

'No.' Enrico shook his head. 'I was born in the
village, but I left as a young man to go into
agriculture. The place was dead: the people were poor
and unemployment was rife. Armando's father,

Ignacio, had emigrated to the Argentine and married there. He was the typical absentee landlord with no interest at all in what was happening back here in Spain. Only at the grape harvest was there any work available locally.' He slanted her a quick look. 'It was my mother who sent word to me that Armando de Montilla had returned to his heritage and was looking for a manager. As a young girl she had worked at the Cortijo in the service of Armando's grandmother, Elena. She was thrilled at the idea that it might at last be restored to its former glory.' He gave a reminiscent smile. 'At first I wasn't interested. I knew from visits to my mother how badly the estate had fallen into decay: but I must admit I was curious to meet the grandson of the legendary Miguel de Montilla. To be honest, I imagined an effete young man as alien to Spain as his Argentinian background, bent only on taking as much profit for as little effort as necessary. I went to that interview prepared to despise him and his ideas.'

'And instead?' Pavane asked softly.

'Instead I met a man who fired me with his own enthusiasm. He saw the Cortijo not so much as a goldmine, but as an oasis which could not only fulfil an innate function, but which by so doing would provide year-long employment to the people of the village.

'He told me his plans to ignore the traditional seasonal crops of vines and olives and to spread the activity of the farm over a number of operations. It was a brave vision and an inspiring one, especially for a young man who knew little about the problems involved.'

'And it succeeded!' Pavane's eyes reflected her own enthusiasm. 'You yourself must take most of the credit for that, surely?'

'You're very gracious, Doña Pavane.' Enrico denied her assertion politely. 'I had the technical knowledge, but Armando had the foresight and the courage of his convictions. He invested a great deal of money in expensive machinery—harrows, ploughs, cultivators, a harvester for the fodder crops—and in those early days he gave as much of himself as of his money. He used to work beside me in the fields, stripped to the waist even in the heat of the day, until his shoulders were burned raw by the sun.'

There was such a wealth of emotion in the older man's voice that Pavane's soft heart responded immediately. 'You think a great deal of my husband, don't you?' she asked softly.

'He's like a second son to me,' Enrico admitted simply. 'Even now, when the estate is prosperous, his interest remains. Armando will never become an absentee landlord and the villagers know it. He's gained universal respect and admiration for what he's brought about in this small corner of Andalusia.'

'But surely one farm can't change the prosperity of a whole village?' Her knowledge of such economics was poor, but if the farm possessed so much modern equipment it would hardly be labour intensive.

'Oh, but it can,' Enrico corrected her politely. 'It has a spin-off effect. Apart from the actual labourers there is work brought about by the other needs of the estate. In some respects it's like a miniature factory, every part of which is profit-making in itself.' He hesitated. 'That's not to say it's one hundred per cent efficient. Armando won't hear of economies being made at the cost of a man's job.'

'A philanthropist?' It was hardly what Pavane had expected to hear of her husband. Surely it was a ruthless spirit that dwelt inside that lean, wickedly graceful, male body?

But Enrico didn't disagree. 'A businessman as well, señora,' he amplified. 'With respect, I would suggest Don Armando exercises a tolerance and understanding towards his employees and in return he demands their loyalty. He'd have no pity for anyone who betrayed him.'

'Are we going to see your house, Don Enrico?' Pablo had stayed silent in deference to his elders for long enough, taking his opportunity of the silence that followed Enrico's last observation to make himself heard.

'I thought we might stop and have some lunch there—if your aunt is agreeable.'

For a moment Pavane was puzzled. Aunt? What aunt? Then she coloured in confusion. Of course, Enrico meant her. Her whole life was so unreal at the moment she'd forgotten she had a relationship with the dark-eyed youngster who was now regarding her with open appeal.

'Can we, Tia Pavane? Oh, can we, please?'

'I would enjoy that very much.' Pavane's eyes thanked Enrico for the invitation, but her mind was busy with what Enrico had said previously. Armando would have no pity. Despite the heat of the day, she shivered. Pity was akin to love, and he had already rejected that emotion. Please God she would never be in a position where she would need compassion from him either!

She pulled herself together with an effort, making a spirited attempt to pay attention as the tour continued, passing through the pasture fields where the newly shorn sheep and herds of cattle cropped from the well-watered ground beneath the shade of strategically growing trees.

Enrico proved an interesting and informative guide, the time passing so quickly that Pavane was shocked to find it was two o'clock by the time they reached the low whitewashed *hacienda* where Enrico and his family lived.

'This is still part of the Montilla land?' she asked in surprise.

'Indeed it is.' Enrico helped her down from the jeep as Pablo jumped lightly to the ground. 'I live here rent free as part of the conditions of my work. Anything I produce within the boundaries of the property belongs to me to do with as I please.' He glanced at her intrigued face. 'You'll find every worker on the estate is given his own plot of ground to cultivate for his own purposes too, as well as being entitled to a share in what the estate produces.'

'I've certainly learned a lot this morning.' Pavane smiled brightly. 'I'm very grateful to you.'

As she followed him towards the *hacienda*, it came to Pavane with a certain knowledge that Armando had not been idly boasting when he had said his name was held in respect locally. Neither, she admitted, would it be an empty deference to his name and wealth. It seemed to her now that her husband had earned the esteem accorded to him. No wonder he had proved so adamant in his desire to protect it!

Lunch consisted of ice-cold gazpacho, followed by a succulent chicken salad, wherein grapes, peppers and orange segments mingled deliciously with finely shredded lettuce and traditional vegetables. Afterwards Enrico's wife, Mariana, served a light vanilla ice-cream followed by home-produced cheese and thin water biscuits. The meal was accompanied by a light fragrant white wine and followed by coffee.

As well as Mariana, Pavane was introduced to Enrico's mother and his son, Esteban, an attractive, pleasant young man who told her he was studying textile design at an art college in Cordoba, but spending the long summer holidays at home with his family.

'A little physical labour in the fields would do him a lot of good,' Enrico remarked goodhumouredly. 'I don't believe those dark shadows under his eyes are due to burning the midnight oil ove his books as he tells me. More likely they're the result of too great a devotion to extra-curricular activities!'

Esteban grinned. 'Do I detect a note of envy, *padre mio*? As a matter of fact I'm not at all averse to a little exercise, particularly in pleasant company.' He turned laughing eyes towards Pavane. 'If Armando is too busy to escort you, I'm at your service, *señora*—name your pleasure—riding, swimming . . .'

'Swimming? You have a pool?' Pavane turned to him eagerly. 'I'd love that!' She ran a hand through her heat-dampened curls. 'I'm not acclimatised to this heat yet.'

'Hardly a pool.' It was Mariana who smiled at her. 'My son's referring to one of the irrigation channels.'

'Oh, but it's super!' Pablo's voice rose excitedly. 'Tio Armando taught me to swim in it last year. It's not very wide or deep, but it goes on for ever. You'd love it,' he assured her happily.

'I guess I would at that.' Pavane's amused glance rested on the eager boyish face. 'You'll have to show me where it is, Pablo.'

'We can all go,' Esteban interposed easily. 'Since our worthy landlord has deprived me of Perico's company, he can hardly object if I find myself other companions in his family, can he?' His laughing eyes flicked from Pavane to his father and back again.

'I'll be your companion. I'll come riding and swimming with you,' Pablo tendered enthusiastically. 'But you won't mind if I bring Tia Pavane with me, will you? You see, when Tio Armando's busy she has to have some other man to protect her—and Tio Armando says he has entrusted her to me!'

A warm pleasure pervaded Pavane. Had Armando really said that to the child? It was a tactful way of ensuring his compliance with her wishes if it were true. She had thought Armando had thrown her in the deep end as far as his nephew was concerned. Now she was touched by his consideration.

'Why, that's splendid, *chico*!' Esteban snaked out a hand to encircle Pablo's slender shoulders. 'To have the pleasure of your company, I'll certainly put up with having your aunt come along too.'

Pavane pulled a face at him. She was used to this kind of flirtatious teasing among students, knowing it to be a harmless game played amongst people who liked each other, but who were otherwise emotionally uninvolved. It certainly didn't merit the stony stare Enrico darted in his direction.

Esteban seemed a pleasant enough young man, and she would welcome some adult company in the difficult days she knew to lie ahead.

CHAPTER SEVEN

IT was past seven when Pavane and Pablo finally returned to the Cortijo.

'Did you like Zarina?' Pablo asked her excitedly. 'I think of all Tio Armando's mares, she's my favourite. I wish I could ride her, but my legs aren't long enough yet.' He looked down at himself in disgust. 'Do you think I'll ever be as tall as Tio Armando?' he asked wistfully.

'Almost certainly,' Pavane assured him. 'Your father's a tall man, isn't he? So I imagine you'll be about his height when you get older.' She nodded with affection at the eager face turned towards her own, 'And yes, I do think Zarina's beautiful—even though she's made my muscles ache.' She rubbed the back of her thighs ruefully. 'It's a long time since I was astride a horse and I'm going to pay the penalty for it if I'm not careful.'

They'd been walking together up the sweeping flight of stairs to the first floor which housed the bedrooms—all seven of them! How fortunate she wasn't going to be responsible for the upkeep of such a place, and how lonely Armando must be living here alone, although she supposed he would entertain a great deal ... She stopped outside the bedroom door, putting a friendly hand on Pablo's shoulder. 'I'm going to have a good soak to stop my muscles stiffening,' she told him. 'So you go along and get yourself ready for dinner and I'll see you downstairs—okay?'

'*Esta bien!*' His face split into an answering grin 'I'm so glad you're here, Pavvy. It's been real fun today!'

Now, at last, she could do what she'd been wanting to do all day. Sitting on the bed, she reached for the phone and dialled the number of the Valmontez vineyard. It was only seconds before she heard Melody's breathless voice.

'Pavane, darling! I've been thinking of you. How—how are things?' Her anxiety came clearly over the phone, but Pavane knew that discretion was essential.

'Everything's fine,' she assured her sister, keeping her voice low and confidential. 'I've had a super day touring all round the estate. I haven't seen all of it by any means, but it's a lovely place, Melody. I know I'm going to like living here.'

'And how is Armando?' The question was loaded with meaning.

'Armando's fine.' Pavane resolutely forbore to mention her growing qualms. 'I haven't seen much of him today because he had to go into Cordoba. But there are no problems, Melody.' Childlike, she crossed the fingers of her free hand behind her back. 'I expect him to be very busy and not spend a great deal of time with me. After all,' she smiled wickedly, knowing Melody would hear the humour in her tone, 'he wasn't expecting to get married quite so suddenly, and it's difficult for him to put off business appointments of long standing.'

'Yes, I see.' Relief showed in Melody's reply. 'I'm so glad you're happy . . .'

Well, 'happy' was hardly the word, but provided Armando kept his distance, Pavane would be well contented in these beautiful surroundings.

'I was hoping we could get together soon, Melly,' she said eagerly. 'Perhaps we could go out riding, Rodrigo wouldn't mind, would he? And I'm going to ask Armando if both of you can come over to dinner some time this week . . .'

'Pavvy darling, I'd have loved to . . . only . . . the thing is . . .'

Oh no! A kind of sick panic rose inside her. Don't let Melody tell her she and Rodrigo had quarrelled again, or worse still, that he suspected the truth! The two of them had seemed so happy on her wedding day at the flamenco. Her sacrifice had seemed so worthwhile ...

'Is anything wrong, Melly?' She couldn't keep the trembling concern from her voice.

'No! No, quite the opposite. Rodrigo wants to take me down to the coast for a week or so. He wants us to have a second honeymoon. He's decided he can spare a few weeks away from the vineyard as long as he's back in time for the vintage. The thing is Pavvy, we're leaving tomorrow.'

'That's marvellous!' Somehow Pavane managed to keep her voice light, refusing to let it echo her growing despair. She'd been depending on Melody's company to help her through the difficult weeks to come. Now she would be alone in an alien environment with no one to confide her hopes and fears to.

'It is, isn't it.' Melody's tone lowered as Pavane sensed her closeness to tears. 'I'm afraid to be too happy, though ...' Her voice tailed off as she struggled for words.

But Pavane needed no interpretation of the silence. 'Don't be scared,' she said gently. 'Nothing's going to spoil your reunion if I can help it. Trust me, Melly.'

The warm bath certainly eased most of her aches and pains. Physically at least she felt quite relaxed as she surveyed the contents of her wardrobe for something suitable to wear. Somehow she must quell this selfish feeling that possessed her that Melody had deserted her. It was nonsense. Her sister had had no option but to go along with her husband's plans. Truthfully she was delighted that events were working out so well for the older girl. With a little groan of self-disgust she wrenched her mind away from her own disappointment. All the evidence told her that Armando was a man of honour. Provided she ignored the wayward reaction of her own untried body towards his incredibly potent masculinity, she had nothing to fear.

She selected a white cotton knit jumper, sleeveless and with a boat neck, teaming it with a plain black circular skirt.

The day in the open air had brought a sparkle to her eyes and a bloom to her cheeks, she noticed critically. She pulled a brush through her curls. Luckily Melody had insisted on her using hair-conditioner so that the blonde ringlets, lightening under the strength of the southern sun, still maintained their glossiness, forming a dramatic foil to her darkened eyelashes and the clear turquoise blue of her eyes. Well, she thought with resignation, the final effect wasn't dramatic—but it would have to do.

As she completed her toilet with a spray of perfume, she wondered what kind of mood Armando would be in. Admitting to herself with a wry grimace at her own timidity that she was glad she wouldn't have to face him alone.

The *sala* was deserted when she entered a few moments later, but the sound of voices from the patio left her in no doubt as to where Armando and Pablo were to be found.

As she walked through the open doors her high heels drew their immediate attention, and Armando rose leisurely to his feet at her approach.

A table had been prepared on the patio itself, and it was obvious they would be dining al fresco. Wrought iron lamps placed at strategic intervals threw a pleasant light over the flower-bedecked area. For the first time she noticed a luxurious swinging hammock lending an air of added opulence to the surroundings.

As her eyes rose from surveying the linen cloth with

its sparkling silver and crystal and its centrepiece of roses and carnations, they locked with Armando's. Moving with an easy and elegant masculine grace, he came towards her. Above slim-cut black trousers he wore an ice-blue shirt, open-necked to reveal the satin skin of his golden, unadorned throat, long-sleeved and cuffed with gold at the wrists. Her heartbeat was a quickening drum in her throat.

'I haven't kept you waiting, have I?' she asked anxiously, staring back into the sable depths of his eyes.

'Not at all,' he replied amicably. 'I made a point of being here early so I could welcome you to your first dinner as mistress of the Cortijo del Rey.'

Before she realised his intention he placed a cool, tanned hand on the top of her bare arm and lowering his head, placed a chaste kiss on her upturned forehead.

Too late to steel herself against his touch, Pavane trembled, feeling a shimmering awareness awakening beneath her sun-kissed skin. Forcibly the memory of those same hands caressing her with a deadly and intimate finesse, returned to torment her.

She gasped, horrified at her own thoughts, trying to release herself before he noticed her furious blush. After all, he had done no more than his husbandly duty before the interested gaze of his young nephew, the untoward rush of blood to her cheeks was absurd. He must have sensed her agitation, for his fingers tightened imperceptibly, his enigmatic eyes gleamed with what could have been amusement or sheer devilry, and without a word he stooped once more to kiss her fully and sweetly on the mouth.

Dazed by the unexpected assault on her lips, she allowed him to lead her to the table and draw out a chair so she could seat herself, smiling brightly at Pablo to mask her confusion: her smile deepening as he told her without pretence, 'I'm glad you've come at last, Pavvy. I'm starving!'

Armando frowned slightly. 'The state of your appetite is not of primary concern to your aunt, I'm sure, *niño*—and by what right do you address her in such a manner?'

The boy's face lengthened at the reproof. Obviously a sensitive child, he had responded immediately to the coolness in his uncle's voice.

'She said I might call her Pavvy.' He threw her a beseeching look before returning his troubled gaze to Armando's solemn face. 'All her very best friends do.'

'I'm afraid being called Tia Pavane made me feel very old,' she confessed, her soft eyes pleading wordlessly on the child's behalf. 'Everyone at home called me Pavvy.'

He gave her a faint smile. 'No doubt you'll let me know when the same privilege will be accorded to me then,' he said drily.

Before she could reply, uncertain as to whether he was teasing or not, one of the young girls who helped Ana wheeled out a trolley.

'Here we are then, *querida*,' Armando continued easily. 'I trust the meal proves to your liking.'

It was delicious. From the delicate seafood cocktail through the veal in cream sauce served with mushrooms and courgettes to the ice-cream garnished with cherries and angelica, Pavane enjoyed every mouthful. Under the influence of the warm relaxing evening air and the excellent Spanish champagne that accompanied the meal, her initial shyness began to fade.

As the evening wore on she found it more and more difficult to retain an air of detachment. She was so full of the day's sights and experiences she found herself chattering on without any thought of whether she might be boring the casually relaxed man who was regarding her with such an attentive, pensive air.

In the midst of rhapsodising about the way Enrico and his family had entertained them, she suddenly froze. How stupid of her to imagine Armando could possibly be interested in her gauche display of naïveté! 'I'm sorry,' she stared down at her lap, cringing inwardly. 'My voice must be getting on your nerves.'

His soft laugh was curiously intimate, instantly reassuring, persuading her to meet his gaze. 'I was just thinking you're more bubbly than the champagne,' he told her gravely. 'I'm delighted you like my home.'

'I love it,' she said from her heart. 'It must give you terrific satisfaction to have created something so worthwhile—so beautiful.'

'Restored rather than created,' he corrected softly. 'But yes, it has been worth all the hard work involved. There's still a great deal more to be accomplished, but by the time I'm satisfied it'll be a worthy legacy to my heirs.'

'You should have sons . . .' She'd spoken without thought, the words sticking in her throat as a cold hard light flared in Armando's eyes turning them to chips of ice.

'Very probably,' he conceded, his tone clipped. 'Fortunately I already have an heir.' He embraced Pablo with a quick glance. 'If I'd intended to found a dynasty I'd have provided myself with a suitable mate long before now.' The dark haughtiness of his expression made her wish more than ever that she had kept her mouth shut. 'I don't believe children should be born for the sole purpose of perpetuating a bloodline or inheriting property!'

Pavane stared back at him, conscious of how his displeasure had quickened her breathing. What did he believe, then? Was he talking about loving relationships? But this was the man who had mocked the very word.

For a moment they sat, eyes locked in conflict. For

heaven's sake, he didn't expect an apology, did he? In the circumstances it had been an obvious comment for anyone to make. Except she wasn't anyone, she acknowledged miserably. She was his wife. She drew a long deep breath. Surely he wasn't imagining . . .

They had both forgotten Pablo's presence at the table. With unenviable timing he dropped his bombshell. 'I expect Pavvy'll soon be having a baby, won't she?' he asked happily, not waiting for an answer. 'Most girls do when they get married, and Papa told Mama that Tio Armando had wasted too much time already. He said . . .'

'What time do you usually go to bed, Pablo?' Pavane interposed quickly before any more gems of wisdom could be repeated. She didn't dare to look at Armando. She only hoped he wouldn't react wrathfully to Pablo's comments, uttered as they had been in total innocence.

'About ten,' he answered her cheerfully, adding ingenuously, 'Would you come up with me when I go?'

'Yes, of course,' she agreed, jumping slightly as Armando's reply bit into her own.

'You're old enough to go up by yourself, *niño*.' His coolness was unmistakable and Pavane felt a trickle of apprehension as she saw Pablo's face drop. 'Run along now and don't trouble Pavane. It's already gone ten.'

She opened her mouth to say it was no trouble, caught the pointed authority directed towards her across the table, and lapsed into silence, but not before she had offered him a glare of mute hostility. Armando nodded curtly to the boy, reinforcing his orders, 'Now, please, Pablo!'

She watched as the boy said his good nights gravely and walked with a dignity beyond his years towards the house, feeling a spurt of hard anger against Armando. She was sure his arbitrary dismissal of his nephew had been brought about by the unknowingly tactless remark about babies. In her opinion such action had been entirely unjustified.

'You want to question my decision?' Armando demanded silkily, giving her a long look, daring her to bring out her challenge into the open.

She forced herself to shrug indifferent shoulders. 'It's a little late for that, isn't it?' She indicated the empty patio. 'I fail to see why I shouldn't go upstairs with Pablo, especially as I'm sure he must be missing his mother dreadfully.'

'I'm sure he is,' Armando agreed, lifting his glass and drinking deeply before continuing. 'And if Dolores hadn't threatened Ramón that once in Brazil, where she has relatives, she would stay there with Pablo and refuse to return to Spain, I daresay my brother wouldn't have insisted on his son remaining in Spain.'

'Dolores threatened to leave Ramón . . . I'd no idea . . .' She looked at Armando's set face, shocked by this revelation of such a shaky relationship between Pablo's parents. 'Why, at our wedding reception Ramón seemed devoted to Dolores!'

'Oh, he is.' There was a harsh intolerance in the statement that shook her. 'Consequently she despises him.' He shrugged dismissively, drawing her eyes to the graceful flexion of his strong shoulders. 'Perhaps now he's taken a firm stand, things may improve between them. Without Pablo's presence he may even be able to persuade her to enjoy a second honeymoon!'

Pavane felt a wicked urge to suggest it must be the honeymoon season—what with Rodrigo and Ramón taking second ones with their wives and she and Armando on their first! Knowing the humour of the matter would totally escape her dark-browed husband, she said meekly instead, 'But Pablo himself must feel rather neglected. Surely a little comfort wouldn't be out of place. Or did you think it too babyish a request?'

'Not at all.' For a moment his face broke into a mischievous smile and she felt the muscles in her stomach tighten alarmingly, an automatic reaction to the fact he was an extraordinarily attractive man when he relaxed. 'It's a remarkably sophisticated request— and one which I was contemplating making myself, to you.'

Holding her breath in alarm, she stared back at his provocative face, seeing the glittering challenge of those cool eyes, the lurking smile that moulded the perfect mouth. He was making fun of her and she should be able to laugh: but somehow she sensed his amusement was only skin deep and beneath it lay the contempt he had demonstrated so forcibly the previous night.

'Ah, well—maybe you're right!' She had made no answer, but he had correctly assumed her total rejection of any such idea. Slowly she expelled her breath as he continued with hardly a pause, 'The night is young yet anyway. Besides, we have the rest of our lives ahead of us.'

Was he deliberately goading her into an argument? She darted him a look, unwilling to enter any arena with him. From that first meeting in the church she had been in no doubt at all of the dangerous ambience of the man now sitting across the table from her, playing so casually with her feelings.

'Certainly we have,' she said at last. 'But not to be spent together.' What she really wanted was to get to her own room, where she would be safe from Armando's contentious presence. 'As for the night being young . . .' She raised the back of her hand to her mouth, smothering a delicate contrived yawn. 'It's been a very full day for me. I can hardly keep my eyes open.'

'I see.' He contemplated her musingly. 'Are you asking my permission to retire, *querida*?'

The lazy impertinence of the question stung her like a nettle. 'I was stating a fact. It hadn't occurred to me I needed anyone's permission to go to bed!'

'Hadn't it?' The straight dark brows winged upward. 'You hadn't considered that companionship has a large part to play in marriage?'

'If the marriage is genuine and the partners compatible—naturally,' she agreed, a growing uneasiness making her voice falter slightly. Surely he didn't mean to force her to sit up half the night with him! 'But it can't be forced,' she went on bravely, 'or it has no value.'

She was uncertain of him in this mood, half-teasing, half-goading her, and she *was* tired.

She saw the half-smile fade from his mouth as his jaw tightened, saw the vertical lines that patterned his taut skin and wished she'd made a more tactful reply.

'So I'd have to force you, would I, if I wanted you to sit next to me on that hammock?' He indicated the gently swinging divan. 'I'd have to exercise brute force if I wanted to sit out under the stars with you, sharing the beauty of the night, drinking brandy with our coffee and getting to know each other better. Is that what you're telling me, Pavane?'

She pushed a nervous hand through her hair with a little sigh, glad that the warm darkness of the evening cast a darker shadow over her pink cheeks. What incredible arrogance she had had to imagine she would be able to handle this impossible Andalusian!

The air was sweet with the scent of flowers and alive with the maraca-like rhythm of the cicadas as they chirruped in the trees. From deep within the walls of the whitewashed *cortijo* came the evocative sound of a radio playing flamenco. It was a night made for romance. Achingly Pavane recalled the warm quiver of expectation that had flowed with the force of an electric current through her body earlier that morning when Armando had embraced her. How dared she place herself in close proximity to him in these quiet and discreet surroundings?

The strange enchanting power he was beginning to have over her was frightening. Suppose she fell in love with him ... to accept his caresses would make her vulnerable in a way that would expose her as a liar and a cheat. If taken to its logical conclusion, it could destroy Melody's happiness for ever.

Even while these thoughts spun through her mind, she realised the other alternative. Armando despised and resented her. He had no real physical desire for her, only the need to hurt and humiliate her because of what she had done. What he *thought* she had done, she amended silently to herself.

The dark eyes that regarded her with cool speculation demanded an answer: His closeness across the table disturbed her, making her pulse race and goose pimples dance across the exposed skin of her shoulders. She fought to control the shakiness of her voice. To show her apprehension might encourage him to increase his provocation, and to defy him might generate the brute force at which he had hinted.

'Certainly I'll sit on the hammock with you if you insist.' She was pleased with the even timbre she produced. 'But, as I said, I'm really very tired. I'd much prefer to get some sleep.' She made an effort to keep her expression bland as she raised eyes the colour of the shallow sea to meet his impersonal stare.

'*Esta bien.*' There was no threat in the easy reply as he stretched lazily, a relaxed sinuous movement of arms and chest that made Pavane aware of how tense her own body was. 'Go get your beauty sleep, Pavanita.' With a seemingly effortless movement he pushed his chair back, regaining his feet and reaching for his brandy glass. 'I'll join you for breakfast in the morning.'

Unconsciously Pavane's fingers tightened round the stem of her empty wine glass as he moved away from her with easy strides, intent on settling his long length on the hammock.

It had been as easy as that! No threats—no persuasion—nothing but a polite acceptance of her request! Hardly daring to believe her luck, she abandoned her grasp on the glass. Walking with a controlled speed, she hastened towards the house, fearful lest he should change his mind and demand her return. She shouldn't have turned, but it was impossible not to. On the threshold she pivoted, her gaze drawn as if by a magnet towards the hammock.

'*Buenas noches*,' came the soft salutation from its depths. 'Sleep well—*esposa mia*.'

In the heat of the late morning sunshine, the balcony that ran the length of her bedroom was deliciously cool. Pavane stood admiring the profusion of flowers covering the wrought iron railings at her side— geraniums, black-eyed Susans, nasturtiums, even hanging carnations rioted in a fantasy of colour against the cool whiteness of their background.

Two weeks had passed since she had used her tiredness as an excuse to seek the lonely comfort of her own room. Two weeks during which Armando had played the courteous, considerate host with style and grace.

Every morning he made a point of breakfasting with herself and Pablo, and she looked forward to the evening meal that always had a sense of occasion attached to it.

Restlessly Pavane poured herself a glass of iced lemon from a flask on the balcony table, taking a long cool sip before standing it down again. There was absolutely no reason for her to feel so unsettled now. Not since Armando had obviously given up the idea of tormenting her with his practised kisses or trying to get some response from her inexperienced body for his own amusement. Since her hasty departure that second night, he hadn't bestowed even one friendly kiss on her. Not even a token peck as a morning greeting.

She smiled ruefully, knowing she was being illogical. It was absurd to resent his indifference. It was what she wanted, wasn't it? She sighed, unable to answer truthfully. It was what she *had* to want. More and more frequently she was wondering how she would have felt if she had met Armando in any other circumstances.

It wasn't that she minded spending the days with Pablo. Often Esteban joined them and together they always found plenty to do to amuse themselves. It was just that she had hoped Armando would make time to come with them on occasions, or even to take her into Seville with him, if only for appearances' sake. But she had been left entirely to her own devices.

Yet it had been only a few days after their first dinner together that he had told her about the financial arrangements he had made on her behalf, brushing aside her protestations that he was being far too generous. 'At least while you bear my name, I expect you to be a credit to me,' he had told her imperiously. 'For God's sake, buy yourself something pretty to wear for the evenings.' His hard glance had assessed her slender body dispassionately, his eyes darkening with some concealed emotion. 'Something long and floaty perhaps . . .' He'd made an empty gesture in the air. 'You might try to look more like a woman than a—a . . .'

'Newly hatched chicken?' Pavane had finished the sentence for him drily, a slight smile curving her lips in an effort to hide the pain the jibe still caused her.

Suprisingly his face had softened, his eyes sparkling with an unexpected mischief that tore at the defences she automatically raised against his charm. 'A very endearing species, Pavanita . . .' The diminutive of her name only emphasised how childish he found her. 'But every bird is more beautiful in its fine adult feathers—no?'

She had nodded her agreement. Like any woman she wasn't averse to dressing well and it would be a considerable triumph if she could make Armando look at her with some appreciation instead of the mixture of disdain, indifference and unwilling awareness that she'd become accustomed to.

But the days had passed and he had made no further mention of her buying clothes. The hope that he would offer to drive her to the nearest towns of Cordoba or Seville never materialised, and she had been too proud to ask it as favour.

Unhappily she wandered back into the bedroom. She still couldn't assimilate totally what had happened to her. How could she possibly have foreseen the devastating effect Armando de Montilla could have on her life? When this ill-fated marriage was dissolved how could she ever find a man to compare with the austere attraction of her husband? Worse still, she knew she would never ever want to try.

She gave a long shuddering sigh, catching her soft lower lip between her teeth. It was ridiculous to speculate about the future, since it was entirely out of her hands. Armando was the master of her destiny and there was nothing she could do about it, except wait upon his pleasure!

Making her way towards the kitchen, she thought again how glad she was she got on so well with Ana. She had been very anxious not to be regarded as an imperious interloper by Armando's staff and her efforts to make friends with the housekeeper had certainly been rewarded by a very happy working relationship.

Not only was she always a welcome visitor in Ana's kitchen, but she found herself learning even more about Armando and the high regard in which he was held locally. It never failed to thrill her when she heard his praises sung. It was as if just by bearing his name, being recognised as his wife, some of the approbation that covered him would rub off on her: would somehow make her more valuable as a person. It was an absurd fantasy, but one which never failed to give her a secret delight.

'Is it all right if I make Pablo and myself a salad?' she asked hopefully, peering inside the large refrigerator.

'Of course, Doña Pavane!' Ana stood by and watched her affectionately as she seized a large plate, quickly building up a colourful array of sliced tomatoes, peppers and cucumbers on a bed of shredded lettuce, adding whole fat sardines and topping the lot with hard, grated cheese, before adding a garnish of black olives as a final touch.

'Not that I like them,' she confided with a grimace, 'but it's more than I dare admit to publicly in this part of the world—and they do make a pretty garnish!'

Producing a freshly baked loaf Ana gave her a tolerant smile. 'And to think a few months ago I was on the point of leaving the Señor's employ . . .' she said, half to herself.

'Leaving?' Surprise mirrored on her face, Pavane stopped in her tracks. 'Oh, but why, Ana?'

'Because I was stupid enough to believe when I heard the Patrón discussing his forthcoming marriage with Don Ramón, that his bride was going to be Isabella Cortez!' Ana made a noise of disgust. 'Now, there's a young madam for you. Beautiful she may be, but spoiled she definitely is—acting as if the Cortijo belonged to her already!' She shook her dark head. 'As much as I admire Don Armando it would have been impossible for me to stay here with Isabella Cortez as mistress of this house!'

Pavane went cold all over as if she'd been flung into a freezing cabinet. Fool that she was, it had never occurred to her that Armando might already have made plans before she was thrust into his life by a furious Rodrigo! Of course, if she hadn't been so anxious about herself, she must have realised. She recalled how pert Isabella had been that day in Armando's office and how tolerant he had been with her. So not only was she, Pavane, an unwanted bride, but she had taken a place already reserved for another woman.

She fought back a wave of nausea, wondering if Armando had explained his reasons to Isabella. Of course, he must have done. She would have been made the exception to Armando's decree of secrecy, in the same way Melody had had to be an exception.

No wonder she had always read such scorn on the Spanish girl's face on their rare meetings!

Absorbed in her own thoughts, she was only vaguely aware that the walls of the room seemed to be closing in on her and her legs no longer seemed strong enough to bear her weight.

CHAPTER EIGHT

'SEÑORA!'

Ana's voice, sharp and concerned, brought Pavane back to the present. 'Señora, you are very pale—are you all right?'

'Yes, yes, of course!' She made a valiant effort to pull herself together as the waves of faintness receded. 'When did you hear this conversation between my husband and his brother?' she asked diffidently, watching the worry fade from the other woman's face as her own colour returned.

'Before I even knew of your existence. Otherwise I wouldn't have made such a silly mistake. Just because Isabella made her intentions towards the Patrón so evident, it certainly didn't mean he shared them—as events proved!' Ana paused while her busy fingers manipulated the coffee percolator. 'It must have been a couple of months ago—when Don Ramón and Doña Dolores were over here discussing their tour to Brazil. Don Ramón was joking, he said something like, "I always thought Dolores would be happier married to you, brother—and I fancy she thinks the same!"' Ana laughed. 'I was just collecting the coffee cups, and Don Armando replied, quite seriously, "As a matter of fact I have my own plans already made in that direction. I shall have an official announcement for you any day now".'

It was as Pavane had thought. A couple of months ago she had never even met Armando. Silently, she piled her salad dish, some plates and cutlery on a tray, making room for the cups and percolator Ana proffered. She had known she must accept Armando's contempt: but no one had warned her she would have to bear the burden of his hatred as well. Surely he must hate her? Not only had she disrupted his life but she had come between him and Isabella—the woman he had planned to make his wife.

Blinded by tears at the full realisation of the situation, she didn't even realise she wasn't alone on the patio until she had put down her tray.

'Have the kitchen staff gone on strike, or is this some game of *Happy Families* you're playing with Pablo, *mi amor*?' The deep, familiar tones drifted across to her.

Jumping at the unexpected sound of Armando's voice, Pavane brushed her tears away with the back of her hand, striving to keep calm.

'Ana lets me get my own lunch,' she confessed, adding unnecessarily, 'I sent Pablo to wash his hands, he'll be here shortly.'

'Good.' Armando rose from the sunbed where he had been reclining his lean length and joined her at the table. 'It looks very colourful,' he said approvingly, eyeing her culinary achievement with signs of amusement lightening the planes of his face. 'Is there enough for three?'

'More than enough.' Ten minutes ago she had been starving; now the emptiness she felt wouldn't be satisfied by food. 'We'll need another plate, though, and I've forgotten the bread . . .'

'Then I'll get them for us,' he said cheerfully. 'It's a long time since I've visited my own kitchens.'

Pavane watched as he strode away, admiring his graceful tight-hipped movement, his lean limbs clothed to advantage in the light blue cotton jean-cut trousers he was wearing, the navy T-shirt emphasising the smoothly muscled expanse of his shoulders and back, before disappearing neatly beneath the leather belt that sat firmly around the dropped waistline of his pants.

The truth was she felt many emotions for Armando de Montilla: admiration, fear, sometimes aggression and a physical reaction that attracted even as it repelled, but above all, despite everything, she suffered an aching hunger to know him better, to hold him once more in her arms, to see him look at her with pleasure. There was an ache in her throat and a stinging behind her eyelids as she admitted her need to herself. She wanted to belong to Armando as the Cortijo did, and the fields and the stock. She wanted him to love her with the same love and purpose and result!

In a moment of passion she had told him she loved him. With the bitter knowledge that his heart was already given to Isabella, she couldn't retract one word of that confession.

Somehow she sat through lunch without drawing undue attention to herself, glad that Armando and Pablo monopolised the conversation. It was only when the meal was finished and her husband said casually, 'I'm taking one of the colts over for Isabella to see,' that she gave any consideration to his unusual presence at the table.

'Could I come with you, Tio?' Pablo's dark eyes sparkled. 'Señor Cortez has a snooker table!'

'Surely you can.' Armando laughed, ruffling the boy's thick hair. 'In fact we've all been invited.'

'Oh, no!' Pavane broke into his sentence before the words had left his mouth. This was the final straw. She needed to come to terms with the facts she had learned from Ana before she could face Isabella with any kind of equanimity. To thrust her into the other woman's company at this moment was fiendish!

'No?' Armando gave her the full extent of his attention, and she felt her whole body tense uncontrollably. Suppose he tried to force the issue, especially as Pablo was regarding her with astonishment? Armando wouldn't want to lose face in front of his young nephew.

'I don't feel . . . that is, I'm not used to this heat . . .' In desperation she tried to find words to excuse herself, striving to keep her dignity beneath his penetrating stare. 'I'd intended resting immediately after lunch,' she finished weakly.

'I see,' he said calmly before turning to Pablo. 'You'd better go and find yourself a clean shirt, *chico*, while I see if I can persuade your aunt to change her mind.'

'I could teach her how to play snooker,' the boy ventured before obeying the instructions and running towards the house.

'Would that be an adequate incentive?' Armando leaned forward to cover Pavane's hand with one of his own, and as she shook her head dismally, added softly, 'No, I thought not. Are you ill, Pavane?'

'No . . . not really . . .' It was impossible to explain how she felt. If he'd wanted her to know about Isabella he would have told her. To admit she felt jealousy was ludicrous, but how else to explain away the sick, pulsating ache in her stomach, the lump in her throat? 'I . . . I . . .' She faltered to a halt, bemused and touched by the unaccustomed concern in his gentle voice.

His strong mouth twisted slightly as the compassion in his tone deepened. 'Ana is concerned about you. She tells me you nearly fainted in the kitchen a while ago. She didn't say it directly, but it's clear she believes you to be in the early stages of pregnancy.' His hand tightened over her own as she gasped her shock.

Closing her eyes, Pavane felt his warmth and vitality seeping through the icy barriers of her mind. 'Are you, Pavane?' His voice was low, expressionless. 'I must know the truth. Was there a mistake? Are you carrying Rico's child?'

She drew a deep shuddering breath, knowing what it must have cost to ask her such a question, because if she were pregnant Armando would find himself tied to her for life. His damaged dreams would die the minute she confirmed it.

'No, Armando,' she said clearly. 'I swear to you I'm definitely not pregnant. It's quite, quite impossible.' Her free hand rose to touch his cheek in a reflex action of comfort and affection. Too moved by what she saw in his eyes, she didn't even hear the indrawn hiss of breath as her soft hand touched his bronzed face. All she saw was the tension leave his face. All she felt was a stab of pain that such a simple denial could bring him so much pleasure. She dropped her hand as if it had been burnt.

'Then as you say, it's probably just the heat.' He paused, his expression brooding and withdrawn. 'You'll be all right if Pablo and I leave you?'

'Yes, of course.' She was relieved at his compliance with her wishes, but then he probably wanted her with him as little as she wished to go. 'I just want to sleep.'

Pavane closed the bedroom door behind her, a heartfelt sigh escaping her trembling lips. After the shock of learning about Isabella the last possibility was that of sleep. At the time marriage to Armando had seemed to provide an ideal escape route for everyone. If only she'd known he was already committed to another woman, she would never have entered so lightly into a mock liaison with him. Now she had to face the unpalatable fact that thoughts and images of her husband were filling her days and a hunger for the touch of his strong body next to hers, disturbing her nights.

Shaken by the strength of her own feelings, she flung herself down on the sun-bed on the balcony. She must hang on to the fact of Melody's happiness. It was the one good thing to come about. Only yesterday she had received a card from her sister telling her how she and Rodrigo had been enjoying the bright lights and excitement along the Costa del Sol before travelling northward to the quieter resorts of the Costa Blanca. Melody had been enthusiastic, and the postcard had been sprinkled with exclamation marks to suggest the superlatives she wouldn't commit to paper.

The next hour passed slowly as Pavane tried to read, finding concentration impossible. If only there was a piano in the Cortijo, she thought wistfully, she could have released some of her tension with a virtuoso performance of a Rachmaninov prelude! Music was a powerful therapy, and although she had aimed to teach rather than to perform publicly she did miss the pleasure of making her own music. At least she had to be grateful that she was able to listen to her tapes and records on Armando's beautiful hi-fi set during the long summer days when she wasn't out exploring.

Her gaze drifted towards the corner of the room where her guitar lay abandoned on a chair. Aware that her mood was too disturbed to be calmed even by its soft magic, she leaned back on the lounger, closing her eyes and hoping she might find sleep: but images of Armando and Isabella together at the Cortez house kept intruding.

Angrily she rose to her feet, furious that her emotions had become so tangled. Perhaps if she went for a walk . . .

The sound of tuneful whistling suddenly became audible above the buzz of cicadas. Leaning over the balcony, she was delighted to see Esteban saunter into view on the patio below. Before she could even call his name he looked up and saw her.

'How about coming for that swim?' he called up to her.

Immediately her spirits lifted. Esteban was a

lighthearted and amusing companion. If anyone could dispel the gloom that was threatening to bury her, he could!

'Love to,' she answered cheerfully. 'Give me ten minutes.'

Somewhere she had a swimsuit fairly new and hardly worn, bought the previous summer when there had been a craze among her friends to go to one of the London swimming pools in their lunch break. Ah yes, here it was.

Quickly undressing, she stepped into the sleek one-piece suit, giving a sigh of relief as the mirror confirmed it still fitted her. Indeed, for a relatively cheap garment it was remarkably flattering, its sunburst effect of scarlet and white stripes emphasising the curves and hollows of her young body. Schoolgirl indeed! Strange how those words still rankled. A mischievous smile curved her mouth. If Armando should ever see her like this he wouldn't think she looked like a newly hatched chicken either!

On impulse she slipped her bare feet into high-heeled sandals and postured before the full-length mirror, one hand on her rounded hip, the other on top of her blonde curls. No, wait a moment . . . the picture wasn't quite right. She selected a scarlet lipstick from the dressing table, applying it thickly to her soft mouth, stressing its curve and fullness, then her eye catching the atomiser of perfume she liberally sprayed it over herself, inhaling the luxurious scent with pleasure. Resuming her pose at the mirror, she said in a bright voice, 'And here we have Miss Cortijo del Rey!'

Suddenly the laughter died from her face. She was no beauty queen. She bore the name of Pavane de Montilla y Cabra, but the reflection that stared back at her was only that of Pavane Calvadene—lost, lonely and—yes, she had to admit it, afraid of what the future might hold for her.

It was only when the sound of Esteban's whistling broke through her reverie that she realised she was keeping him waiting. Quickly she stepped into a tiered scarlet skirt of Indian cotton, grabbed a large bathtowel and left the room without a backward glance.

The irrigation channel proved as delightful as Pablo had promised. Carved out of the rocky soil and lined with concrete, fed by a clear cold spring, it was exhilarating and refreshing. Each side of its width, paving stones had been set and beyond these grew a mixture of coarse grass, interspersed with cacti and succulent plants.

On the side nearest to the Cortijo, Armando had had a long shelter built. That it was frequently used was evident from the garden furniture lying beneath its shade in sprawled abandon. That afternoon, however, only Pavane and Esteban shared the beauty of the quiet spot.

After half an hour the chill of the spring water was making her flesh come out in goose pimples despite the air temperature. Clambering out, she selected a sun-lounger, pulling it out into the sunshine and covering it with her towel. The sun would soon dry her costume and dispel her shivers. Lying back, she abandoned herself to its warm caress.

'*Dios*, Pavane! How on earth did that happen?' Esteban's voice broke into her daydreams at the same time as she felt his hand lightly traverse one of her thighs.

She hadn't heard him approach, his bare feet silent on the hot concrete. Now he sprawled out on the ground at her side, his fingers following the line of a dark bruise with horrified amazement.

A smile dimpled her cheeks. 'Playing football with Pablo and you the other day.'

'God, my father would kill me if he knew!' he said

feelingly. Pavane suppressed a grin at his reaction. No longer the suave young man, he was very much the recalcitrant son. His hand still covering the mark as if by hiding it he could deny any responsibility for its presence, he asked wonderingly, 'However did you explain it away to Armando?'

'She hasn't—yet!' Armando's voice had a whiplash quality as it shattered their complacency.

He must have approached them through the belt of trees behind the shelter and neither of them had heard his catlike advance, nor had their eyes, fixed as they were on Pavane's slender curvaceous leg, observed his passage towards them.

Immediately Esteban sprang to his feet, looking oddly guilty, which was absurd because he must realise he wasn't responsible for her actions and if she got bruised playing football then it was entirely her own affair. There was no logical reason for the look of apprehension which now coloured Esteban's pleasant features.

Pavane swung her legs over the side of the lounger as Armando walked round to face them both. For the first time she saw the expression on his face and her heart sank. Whatever had happened at the Cortez *hacienda* had brought him no joy. Perhaps he and the lovely Isabella had quarrelled. She hadn't expected him back so soon. Looking at the stern unbending lines of the handsome face that could quicken her heartbeat and turn her legs to gelatine, she was filled with a dreadful foreboding.

Before she could think of anything to say to lighten the tension that hovered over them, Armando's dark eyes flickered over Esteban's still wet form. Beneath the pensive, arrogant gaze of the older man, Esteban stooped to pick up his towel.

'Your father needs you in the office.'

It was a statement that allowed no appeal, and

Esteban knew better than to argue. He had been dismissed from the scene as clearly as if Armando had ordered him to leave.

He shrugged his shoulders and clambered into his jeans, pulling them over the still damp bathing trunks and flinging his towel defiantly round his neck.

'Sorry, Pavane—but you see how it is . . .'

Yes, she was beginning to see how it was: but she didn't know why. From Armando's stance, rigid with aggression, she was sure she was going to find out.

'Get your clothes on!'

Pavane winced as the words flailed her. Anyone would think she looked indecent! Her hands were none too steady as she reached for the scarlet skirt and adjusted its elasticated waist round her slender middle. You could search the length and breadth of Spain and not find a more proper bathing costume than hers, she thought mutinously, conscious of the disapproval on every line of Armando's face as he watched her, his eyes narrowed, his mouth a taut line of displeasure.

'You have shoes, I presume?'

Her nerves tightened beneath his harsh tones as reaching for the spindle-heeled sandals she clung stubbornly to the silence that protected her pride. She had never seen him in such a foul mood and she had no idea what to do to appease it.

Her fingers trembled as she finally fastened the ankle straps and stood quietly awaiting the next instruction. A hard muscle was clenching spasmodically in his jaw as he regarded her, his face a taut still mask of anger, his eyes dark and dangerous beneath heavy lids. Then his hand reached out, taking her firmly by the upper arm, his fingers biting painfully into the soft flesh as she suppressed a whimper of pain.

Without speaking he pushed her forward, making

for the path through the trees which led to the wider track where he had parked the jeep. He made no allowance for the fact that she was wearing high heels which shortened her stride, making the rough terrain dangerous to her. On several occasions only the firm grip he maintained on her arm prevented her from falling, so it was almost a relief when he pushed her inside the jeep and she could sit down.

Unable to stand the silence any longer, she turned on him heatedly. 'I suppose you'll tell me what this is all about eventually?' Her fingers massaged the bruised skin of her upper arms.

'I'll spell it out for you word by word,' he promised bitterly. 'As soon as I get you home—never fear!'

But she *was* beginning to fear: and home! That was a laugh. The Cortijo was where she was staying temporarily—an unwanted encumbrance. Never once had she thought of it as home. She lapsed back into silence. It was neither the time nor the place for remonstrance.

Vainly trying to subdue the panic which was now filtering through her whole system, she made no effort to fight him when, having arrived at the Cortijo, he again took her by the arm and half led, half pushed her up the stairs.

It was only when Armando thrust her through the door of her bedroom, and kicked it closed behind both of them that she twisted round, attempting to escape the brutal hold of his fingers as her eyes flickered defiantly over the hard chiselled lines of his face.

'So!' The brilliant sparkle of his dark eyes taunted her. 'All this talk of not being used to the heat was just an excuse to keep your assignment with Esteban!'

Shock kept her momentarily silent as Armando's accusation branded her a liar. 'How long has it been your practice to provide a cabaret for my farmhands and their relations, I wonder?' His lip curled in mocking derision as he scanned her lightly clad body.

It was bitterly unfair, and he must know it. Indignation fought with compassion for what he must have suffered at Isabella's hands to force him so far from the path of justice.

'It's the first time I've ever been swimming there.' Pavane kept her voice under control with an effort. 'I'd no idea you'd object, because Esteban is the son of one of your employees.' She looked challengingly into his lean angry face, feeling her throat constrict as her pulse beat quickened; alarmed as much by her own temerity in arguing with him as by his reaction to her stand.

His cruel gaze glinted over her upturned face. 'I object because he's a man!'

She stared at him in disbelief, experiencing a growing, heart-racing fear about what he meant to do to her. For what did she really know about this man who legally and in the sight of God held jurisdiction over her?

'He's a boy!' she protested through dry lips.

'He's nearly as old as Rico!' Accusation and contempt lay like twin souls in the bitter depths of his harsh voice.

'You don't imagine . . . you can't think . . .' Words of denial froze on her lips.

'You lied so you could meet him—and it wasn't the first time, was it? I understand you've been seeing a great deal of him.'

'It's no secret.' She resented having to justify herself and an edge of spirit crept into her voice. 'Yes, I've seen him. He's a good friend to Pablo and me!'

'*Is* he?' There was a note of menace in the soft reply. 'Did you forget what I told you about behaving with discretion, *amada*?' He raised his hand to stroke her face with studied gentleness.

'Stop it, Armando!' She shivered beneath the deliberately sensual caress of his possessive fingers, aware they belied their impression of love. 'Isn't it enough you forced me to marry you, however temporary it may be, without trying to prevent me from having friends?'

'No, it's not enough!' Pavane stiffened beneath the keen penetrating gaze that burnt into her defences. 'And *I* forced you into nothing. You forced yourself into marriage by your lack of self-control, your immorality and the contempt you showed for your brother-in-law's hospitality. You made it impossible for Rodrigo, who is a man of honour, not to demand that my brother wed you. Because I didn't want to see Rico's life ruined by your self-indulgence and promiscuity, I took over the role of protecting the honour of our family name. That makes me entitled to your total loyalty until such time as I'm legally rid of you!'

Pavane sucked in her breath in a sobbing gasp, recoiling as if from a blow beneath the scathing condemnation, her lips parting from the shock of his onslaught. There were strange fires burning in the midnight depths of his accusing eyes as he dared her to excuse herself. Self-indulgent and promiscuous indeed! The words seared her self-esteem, goading her beyond logic and common sense.

For a split second his attack had stunned her, now she wanted only to retaliate. To hurt him as deeply as he had wounded her.

'What family honour?' she bit back at him. 'Your infamous grandfather married for money and left a statue of his mistress posing as the Madonna: and your father cared so little for his inheritance he became a parasitic absentee landlord! And *you* dare to speak to *me* of honour!'

She turned angrily on her heel, shaking with a

mixture of fury and fear at her own boldness, anxious to put the width of the bed between them, spinning to face him again as she reached the far wall, curiosity and apprehension marking her face with their presences.

Armando stood still where she had left him, looking every inch a man without compassion: his face proud and autocratic as the Moorish princes who had left the stamp of their race on his ancestors, paler than usual, the dark brows straight-winged above eyes glittering with a pain that promised her no mercy.

His silence terrified her more than his insults. Every nerve in her body quivered as he let out a deep sigh and moved across the room towards her. Certain now he would strike her, Pavane still continued to face him bravely, flinching mentally from the blows her imagination told her she had earned. She had offered him a dreadful insult when she derided his family. There was no way she could expect leniency.

When he lifted his hand she could no longer face the smouldering passion etching itself on every line of his lean, audacious countenance. She closed her eyes, turning her cheek to rest on the wall behind her, she resigned herself to accept retribution.

When she felt his mouth take open-lipped possession of her own, when she smelled the sweet, sun-washed scent of his skin, when she sensed the burning heat of his flesh reaching to embrace her cold, shivering body, she thought she must be hallucinating. Strong arms enfolded her, drawing her away from the wall where she had taken refuge, clasping her against his own virile form, crushing her breasts against his chest, her thighs against the muscled hardness of his own.

Was this forgiveness, then? Her startled eyes flew open in wordless gratitude that he should have regretted the epithets he had hurled at her and overlooked her heated retaliation.

It was then she read his purpose. Even to her inexperienced eyes his ragged breathing, the glowing heat of his ardent body, the soft dark-pupilled eyes, the insistent pressure of his hard mouth, spoke their own terrifying message.

Pavane tore her mouth away from his embrace, her hands lifting to seize the sides of his face in an effort to force it away from her own. But he was far too strong for her puny efforts, his questing lips moving in a slow, greedy enjoyment of her cheek.

'Armando—no!' she cried piteously, the horror of imminent rape staring at her like a spectre, but she was a prisoner in the firm circle of his arms.

'Pavane—yes!' he mocked her, his voice heavy and slurred. 'Come on, my angel, it's not as if I were the first man to enjoy your delectable body . . .'

Desperately aware of her own vulnerability, she was taut as a highly tuned violin string, she tried to dissuade him, her trembling fingers clutching at his waist.

'That's right,' he muttered. 'Touch me, hold me, *querida*. Here . . .' He jerked his T-shirt free from the confining belt and her fingers were forced to touch the warm naked flesh that pulsed beneath it.

'We can't . . . we mustn't . . .' she pleaded, anguish sharpening her words. 'The annulment . . . you promised me an annulment!'

She heard Armando's breath rasp as he pulled away slightly to stare down into her pleading face. 'But then, my sweet, as you've so forcibly reminded me, my family isn't noted for its ideals of honour. What value is the promise of a man with a background like mine?'

Oh, dear God, what had she done? Armando had returned home frustrated and angry after his meeting with Isabella and she had goaded him into using her as a substitute for the outlet of his aroused passions.

Wildly she cried out, 'You don't want *me*. You only want to punish me . . . Armando, I beg you . . .' Her voice stalled on a sob.

'I've wanted you from the first moment I set eyes on you.' Softly emphatic, the words forced her to meet his magnetic gaze, her eyes widening at what she read there. 'For weeks I'd suspected Rico had formed an unsuitable alliance. It was a mixture of duty and curiosity that brought me to the church on that first occasion I saw you.' He paused, transfixing Pavane with the depth of emotion that emanated from him, causing his body to tremble. When he continued his voice was thick and husky with unconcealed desire. 'Afterwards I waited outside and saw you walk into the bright light of the morning with Perico at your side. I had to face the truth. In church I'd used the power of prayer to crush the temptation the sight of your lovely face had offered me. Now I have nothing to protect me. I saw the woman who had captivated my youngest brother—and I wanted her for myself!'

Not me! she wanted to cry out. It wasn't me Perico wanted! But all she could do was shake her head in silent negation, stunned by the painful confession that spilled from Armando's twisted lips.

'Oh yes,' he continued harshly, 'I wanted you then, and I've wanted you ever since. At one time I thought if I brought you here I could get you out of my system—but it hasn't worked. If it means we stay married for life—then it's the price I'm prepared to pay!'

Before she guessed his intention he slid his hand beneath the top of her swimsuit, drawing it gently down to reveal the cool glistening orbs of her pale breasts.

She heard his sharply indrawn breath, knew an inexplicable pleasure and excitement that he could get such joy from the sight of her body, then his hands were cupping their thrusting beauty, his thumbs beginning to trace the delicate pink aureoles that mantled their loveliness.

'I can't pay that price!' The cry was wrung from her as she felt her body begin to melt beneath his loving caress.

But her protest was ignored as Armando lowered his dark head to bestow a gentle kiss on each crushed-rose tip in turn. 'You don't have the choice.' With a sudden movement he pushed the band of her skirt over her hips, letting the scarlet cotton drift to the floor.

'Don't do this to me, I implore you . . .' She was reduced to pleading, uncaring that she must abase herself verbally before him. Anything rather than that he should take her in lust and tie himself to her for the rest of their lives.

Even the problem of Melody faded before the thought of her own violation. The fact that the love she felt for Armando was already wreaking its own magic on her body had escaped her notice. All she could think of was that she was being used as a substitute for Isabella, and the prospect revolted her.

'Whatever we do, we do together,' Armando's soft voice murmured against her hair. 'Don't pretend to be indifferent, my lovely wife—your sweet body betrays you. You were made for love, *querida*—we both know that. Who better than your lawful husband to become your lover? Come on, *mi amor*, enough of these games . . .' His voice was softly persuasive, huskily pleading. 'Undo my belt, Pavane, help me . . .'

'What!' She tried to step back, only to find herself hard up against the wall. Despite his threat that she had no choice, it was clear he wanted her willing participation.

'My belt,' he repeated patiently nodding down at his waist. 'Undo it, please, my love.' He swung his arms up, trapping her in their circle. Her eyes slid down to the strip of leather encircling his body an inch or so beneath his supple, firm waist. Wordlessly she shook her head. To touch him would be the first step on the path that would lead to her own destruction.

He smiled a soft, knowing smile. A heartbreaking interaction of eyes and mouth that made the blood run like fire in her veins. Then his lips were against her own, kissing her with open-mouthed eagerness, transmitting the mounting passion that made his strong body tremble to her own responsive slender frame.

Fresh torment surged through Pavane as she felt that response and gasped aloud with the awareness of her own arousal. Before she could regain her senses he had released her to drag his T-shirt clear of his head, returning almost immediately to his previous position. Now their flesh mingled: hers cool from swimming, his burning with a passion that was impossible to conceal.

With a little moan, Pavane clasped her hands about him, unable to resist the lure of his warm golden skin, feeling his heated body quiver beneath her cool touch as he groaned deeply repeating her name like an incantation: 'Pavane—Pavane . . .'

Caught up in something beyond her control, wanting only to ease his torment, she trailed her hand down his ribs, knowing it wasn't the coolness of her hands that made him shudder.

Suddenly she was doing what he had asked of her. Nothing had prepared her for the heady awakening of sensuality in her own nature, or the way it was mutating her own body. Her need to touch him was pervading her whole being, as she surrendered to the clamour of her senses, feeling his body grow rigid as she slid the leather belt from its fastening.

His hands tightened painfully round her breasts, his thumbs moving rapidly to excite her beyond tolerance.

Filled with an aching need for a fulfilment she could only imagine, her hands began to move without inhibition over his body as the last murmur of common sense was burned in the fever that consumed her.

'Go on—*mi amor*——' Armando's dark tones were a verbal caress to her ears. 'Go on, my sweet love. Don't stop now!'

CHAPTER NINE

OBEDIENTLY, shaking because Armando's desire was infiltrating itself through every fibre of his being where it touched her own, Pavane slipped the clasp at his waist. As if in a trance her cool fingers pushed the material away from his lean hips. Instantly, he kicked himself free of its encumbrance, and with a smooth movement divested her of the swimsuit, gathering her naked and trembling into his arms to deposit her gently on the bed.

Hardly aware of her own nakedness, Pavane gazed at him, her heart in her eyes. She could think of nothing now except the promise latent in the powerful lines of his long shapely limbs, the breadth of his unclad shoulders, the strong lines of his flat stomach and neat waist.

She held her arms out to embrace him, knowing she was hopelessly caught in a mesh of intrigue that could destroy so much happiness, but totally unable to resist him. There was no room for thought as Armando's body entwined with hers and she experienced the piercing ecstasy of his mouth as it traced a line of passionate kisses towards her breasts. She moaned deep in her throat as his hands slid down her body with their gentle intimate touch.

His name was on her lips, her heart beating too rapidly, her breathing too laboured to enable her to murmur it aloud when with his face buried between her tender breasts, Armando stilled his caresses.

One moment he was an ardent, attentive lover. The next he was pushing her away, levering his naked legs over the edge of the bed. Puzzled and discomfited,

Pavane struggled to sit up. Had her inexperienced response disappointed him? Had she taken too much without giving? In her innocence she had been hesitant to fondle his smooth skin with the deeply intimate caresses he had bestowed on her.

Then the yawning ache of initial disappointment was followed by a surging sense of relief that for whatever reason he had been strong enough for both of them. She had had a lucky escape, and when her traitorous body had regained its composure she would be able to acknowledge her good fortune.

She tried to quell her feeling of inadequacy, finding it impossible to look at him as she drew the bedcover across to conceal her nakedness. Perhaps her inexperience hadn't been to blame. Perhaps her earlier anguished pleading had reached through to him, perhaps he had simply realised she wasn't the woman he loved, perhaps he'd found it not so easy to relinquish the pride he had in his honour after all, perhaps . . .

'You make it impossible!' There was a vicious sting in the angry words he hurled at her. She *must* have done something wrong! In an agony of embarrassment she cowered to conceal herself from his accusing eyes.

With a sharp furious movement Armando turned away from her. Hardly believing what she was seeing, she stared in amazement as he seized the glass atomiser of perfume from the bedside table and pacing with the lithe graceful strides of a jungle cat towards the balcony, sent it crashing down on to the patio below.

'Why!' One word displayed her deep shock and distress as she quailed before the force of his pent-up rage.

'Because you make it impossible for me to forget that other men have enjoyed your body when you offer yourself to me drenched in the perfume they've carried away on their bodies after taking their pleasure with you!'

'But Kevin and I . . .' Pavane couldn't finish the sentence, because she'd never mentioned Kevin to him. Certainly not told him the perfume had been a gift from a boy-friend. She bit her lip in confusion, flinching before the antagonism directed towards her.

'Kevin?' he laughed bitterly. 'How many names are there on the list, I wonder?' He came towards her, his face coldly accusing. 'No, the lover I referred to was Rico—my brother Rico—bruised and bleeding because he'd succumbed to the poison in your eyes: and what a poison they carry!'

Pavane swallowed deeply, choking back on her tears, unable to speak beneath his heavy scorn, watching the cruel words drop from the beautiful mouth that had winged her on a pathway to the stars only to abandon her.

'He looked as if he'd escaped from Hell, but the evidence of Heaven wasn't easily overlooked.' Armando moved his head in a gesture of disgust. 'His face, his hair, were imbued with perfume—your perfume. It was a scent that lingered in the room, conquering even the smell of antiseptic with its potency!'

Helplessly Pavane stared at her hands, remembering how Perico's head had fallen against her breasts.

'And this afternoon,' there was a shimmering anger in Armando's voice, 'you painted your beautiful mouth, put on ridiculous shoes and bathed yourself in the same perfume. Why, Pavane? To go swimming with a *friend*?'

They had come full circle. She closed her eyes in desperation. There was nothing she could say to satisfy him now. She didn't see him stoop to gather his discarded clothes, but when she heard him walk to the door and pause, she turned her empty eyes towards him, hoping for something, anything that would indicate he didn't totally despise her.

'Perhaps it's just as well you like to go to your lovers so sweetly perfumed.' Icy disdain glazed the dark eyes. 'If the aura hadn't been so evocative, I might easily have added to their number. Your outward purity has a deceptive quality about it which could make fools of better men than me!'

The door closed behind him. Pavane was alone: shivering as if she had an ague, burning as if she had a fever.

'I'm bored, Pavvy.' Pablo stood in front of her as she swung to and fro in the hammock, an unopened book in her lap. 'Isn't there something exciting we could do?'

Pavane returned his gaze, evaluating with a sense of pleasure the still childish beauty of his face. Even now with the evidence of his declared boredom apparent in his frown and the slightly petulant drift of his mouth, he was a remarkably attractive boy, the family likeness of the Montillas clearly perceptible. With manhood the pre-puberty softness of that face would take on the hard-boned look of his father and Armando. The soft mouth would keep its perfect outline, but would lose the feminine sweetness of a young boy.

'Isn't there, Pavvy?' The insistent young voice demanded a reply. 'We haven't even seen Esteban for ages now. Enrico says he's still at the *hacienda*, but he's got a lot of studying to do. Do you suppose we could go over and see if he's finished it yet?'

'I don't suppose he'd be pleased if we interrupted him,' Pavane answered hesitantly. There was no doubt in her mind that Armando had been responsible for Esteban's sudden disappearance from the scene. Dared she try to rekindle their friendship and risk antagonising Armando? After all, it was nearly a fortnight since that dreadful afternoon. The absurdity of his accusation still angered her, and she burned with the frustration of not being able to justify herself in a better light. She sighed deeply. If she had guessed at the beginning that the time would ever come when she longed for Armando's good opinion and his respect, she would have begged Rodrigo to send her back to England. It would have been better to be penniless than have to suffer her husband's cold indifference.

For Armando had become a stranger to her. No more did he share breakfast with them, and the familiar evening meal, still taken outside in the warm night air scented with the fruit and flowers of Andalusia, had become an ordeal. So oppressive was the atmosphere that Pavane had got into the habit of retiring as soon as it was finished, going upstairs with Pablo, her withdrawal always unchallenged.

After seeing the child settled in bed, she had spent most evenings either reading a book from Armando's extensive library or finding comfort from playing her guitar, attempting to soothe her jangled nerves with the poignant, emotion-evoking melodies which so suited its beautiful mellow tones.

Mostly it had been in vain, the music of her choice only serving to agitate the nameless longings that tormented her, rather than to stultify them.

In those hot Spanish nights, sleep never came easily to her. Armando had spoken to her of his desire and the memory of his fervent body, the ardour of his lovemaking, tortured her emotionally and physically as she tossed and turned into the small hours.

She wasn't so naïve as to imagine his desire was linked with love for her. No, it was clear that the strain of celibacy, when he had a nominal wife at his pleasure, was proving more difficult to cope with than he had anticipated. His impassioned words spoke only of the urgent needs of a virile and vital male body at the peak of its power. She shuddered, remembering how she had ceased to be a rational human being beneath his touch, how she could have sacrificed Melody's happiness—her entire future—in her mindless acceptance of the man she had married under false pretences.

It had been Armando's pride, his conceit that had pulled her back from that precipice. He hadn't been able to bear the thought that Perico had known her body before him. The belief that his young brother had enjoyed her had been a burning and unremitting torture, eroding his complacency. He wouldn't stoop to sample what he believed Perico had been allowed to take so easily!

'Well, could we ride over to Enrico's place? Last time I saw him, he promised me a book of cuttings he's got about Real Madrid.' Pleading brown eyes begged her consent as Pablo interrupted her introspection.

Would there be any harm in it? Armando had put no actual restrictions on her movements, neither did he ever ask what she had done during the day or where she had been. Mariana and her mother-in-law would certainly be at the *hacienda*, so even if he did find out, he could hardly accuse her of a secret assignation.

Pavane made her mind up briskly. 'Yes, I don't see why not.' Flinging her book down, she jumped to her feet. 'Race you to the stables!'

It was a pleasant ride, but it was clear from the coolness of Mariana's reception that Pavane wasn't a welcome visitor.

'My son's not here,' she said coldly, not deigning to amplify the statement.

'It's not important.' Pavane tried not to appear hurt by Mariana's attitude. 'It's just that he promised

Pablo a book and we haven't seen him for some time, so Pablo wondered if he might collect it.'

'He may certainly see if he can find what he wants in my son's room.' Mariana indicated a door and watched until Pablo disappeared inside it, before turning her set face back to her guest. '*Señora*, my son is young and easily impressed. Also he lacks discretion, but I'm sure he wouldn't intentionally wish to offend you.' She tilted her chin defensively.

'Of course he hasn't offended me,' Pavane protested in amazement. 'I've enjoyed his company very much—both of us have!'

Mariana stared back at her with unblinking eyes. 'Don Armando gave Enrico the impression that Esteban had become a nuisance to you.'

'Oh, no . . .' Dismayed, Pavane bit her lip.

'You understand, *señora*, that Enrico's whole existence is here at the Cortijo del Rey. It would break his heart were he to be dismissed.'

'Enrico—dismissed?' Pavane couldn't stop the mounting horror in her voice. 'Why ever should Enrico be dismissed?'

'You mean you don't realise that Don Armando would discharge his manager without a qualm if his wife had been insulted by just one member of that manager's family?'

'I think there's been some misunderstanding.' Unhappily Pavane shook her shining head. 'In the first place I regarded, still do regard, Esteban as my friend. If my husband has given you the impression that this isn't the case, I can only assume Armando is under some misapprehension.' She paused, wondering how far she dared to assume responsibility for Armando's intentions, then continued bravely, 'In the second place, I believe my husband has more integrity than to dismiss someone he trusts and admires as a friend in any circumstances.'

Mariana's expression softened marginally. 'Don Armando is a just and generous man, but a *man* above all. One who would defend what is his to the very gates of Hell—perhaps even beyond. Forgive me,' there was a muted eloquence in her dark eyes, 'but had you considered that it might be your very avowal of friendship for my son which has disturbed the Patrón?'

'But that would be ridiculous!'

'Not ridiculous for a man with a young and lovely wife, who thinks every other man must see her through the passion-glazed windows of his own eyes.'

Pavane shook her head in silent denial. Impossible to explain that Armando regarded her with contempt rather than love and was only intent on seeing she didn't disgrace his name. It was incredible that he should have vented his anger with her on Enrico's family. It made her position impossible.

'I can see it was a mistake to come here this afternoon,' she said with a quiet dignity. 'Please be assured I shan't do so again—and please don't worry. I'm certain my husband would never act dishonourably towards any member of your family.'

For the first time Mariana smiled. 'Jealousy is a powerful emotion. It can tear even the strongest man apart, make him act out of character.' She hesitated, then sighed. 'To live with his jealousy must be a small price to pay for the joy of holding Armando's heart in your hand, *señora*—but I beg you, never provoke it or exploit it even for amusement—because in this country, a man's emotions run deep as the life-giving springs that bless our land, and by such actions, tragedies are born!'

How well she knew it! Pavane nodded in silent acceptance. How wonderful it would be to hold Armando's heart in her hand, she thought wistfully.

'And now, *señora*, allow me to offer you some refreshment before you and the child leave.'

Gratefully Pavane accepted the fresh orange juice proffered, sitting on the terrace sipping it while Mariana went in search of Pablo.

'Pavvy, look what I've got!' Pablo's eager voice made her turn her head a few moments later. Under one arm he held a large book. In the other clasped against his chest was a football. 'Would you play with me, Pavvy?'

'What, now?' She raised startled eyebrows. 'Heavens, no! Not in this heat.'

'Well, later, then,' he persisted. 'We could go back to the Cortijo and stable the horses, then we could walk over to one of the far pastures and have a game there. Oh, go on, Pavvy, please!' Dark eyes pleaded with all the charm the years had bred into the Montilla men. 'I've got no one else to play with, have I? Esteban doesn't come and see us now, and Tio Armando is always too busy ... please?'

'Girls aren't supposed to play football,' Pavane protested weakly, but she felt guilty because of the absence of Esteban. She was already weakening, and the boy knew it.

'But *you* do—you're not like other girls,' he told her winningly. 'They don't know how to have fun. They wouldn't wrestle and climb trees with me like you've done. You're as good as any boy!'

Despite herself Pavane felt her face breaking into a grin. To be likened to one of the superior sex was just about the greatest compliment that Pablo's young mind could encompass, and as such she found it irresistible. Besides, the sheer physical effort was just what she needed to work off the growing tension her strained relationship with Armando was engendering.

'One last time, then,' she compromised, and was rewarded by his uplifted mouth and sparkling eyes which did not quite hide the smug satisfaction lurking behind them. But then he was growing to manhood and learning the subtle ways of imposing his will on the weaker sex. In another ten years he would be a force to be reckoned with, she acknowledged silently. She hoped for his sake that Ramón and Dolores would stay together to give him a settled home environment. It might prevent him from making the same mistakes as his uncles: Perico's one of passion—Armando's one of pride.

'We must go back now, *chico*. By the time we reach the Cortijo it'll be gone eight!' Pavane hadn't realised how quickly the time had flown until the fading light had forced her to look at her watch. Now she stared at it in horror. 'I'll have to have a bath, and your uncle's not going to be too pleased if we keep him waiting!'

That was an understatement, and she knew it. In Armando's present mood he would find fault with any deviation from his instructions, however slight.

'All right,' Pablo agreed graciously. 'But I'm a good player, don't you think? Perhaps I might play for Spain one day.'

'Perhaps.' Pavane slid her eyes over his slim yet sturdy figure, marvelling at the universal dreams of young men. Her gaze returned to her own body and she grimaced. She had allowed Pablo to persuade her that she should dress suitably for the game, donning an old pair of shorts she had cut down from jeans and topping them with a well-worn white T-shirt, completing the picture with an old pair of trainers. Added to which, the field had been under the sprinkler and there had been patches of ground still damp. Once or twice she had skidded to her knees, and her long legs in the abbreviated shorts showed evidence of her tumbles.

'Your knee's bleeding.' Pablo had followed the direction of her own eyes and was regarding the trickle of blood with interest. 'Does it hurt?'

'Not much.' It hadn't until the last few moments. Now it was beginning to throb and tremble. Still, it was nothing a good warm bath and a plaster wouldn't cure. She rubbed it gingerly with her fingers. 'Don't worry, you won't have to carry me back!' She ran her hands across her face, wiping away the glow of perspiration that her efforts had induced. 'Come on, Pablocito—I'll race you back to the Cortijo! Let's see if we can make it before your uncle sees us!'

Pavane had longer legs, but Pablo had surprising speed, and far from having to hold herself in check, Pavane found herself having to sprint as hard as possible to keep in touch with him. In the event, he was a good ten yards clear of her as he broke through the surrounding screen of trees and burst on to the patio.

If she had been concentrating less on catching him, or even if she had been moving at a slower speed, she would have realised that the patio was full of people before her sudden arrival precipitated her within yards of them.

Her frantic and horrified gaze took in Isabella Cortez, beautifully gowned in a long white cotton dress, sprinkled with scarlet poppies, the off-the-shoulder neckline displaying her smooth brown skin; her lustrous hair a bouncing mass on her shoulders.

She also recognised Isabella's parents, Señor and Señora Cortez, who had been guests at her wedding. Additionally there were three other people she had never set eyes on before: an elderly elegantly dressed man who was regarding her with some surprise, another beautifully dressed woman seated beside him and a young man, probably in his twenties, who was gazing at her with a mixture of amusement and frank admiration as his eyes travelled slowly down her panting form.

Lastly there was Armando, whose eyes she daren't

meet. Of Pablo there was no sign, and she could only assume he had taken discretion as the better part of valour and dashed straight through to the house without waiting for introductions. If only she might dare to do the same! But Armando had risen to his feet and was coming towards her, his face devoid of expression.

Like a frightened animal's her eyes darted quickly around for a means of escape, but there was none. Behind Armando's approaching form she saw the other men rise to their feet and knew she would have to brazen it out.

Formally dressed in a light suit, her husband moved with the unaffected grace of movement that could still make her catch her breath. As he grew nearer Pavane perceived the cold displeasure sitting like a mask on the proud Latin lines of his face. Knowing what a spectacle she had made of herself before his friends, she felt as humiliated as he must do on her behalf.

As if sensing her desire to escape, he placed a firm arm round her shoulders, drawing her inexorably forward. Standing there, immaculate in dress and manner, every inch the master of the Cortijo del Rey, he introduced her to Señor and Señora Abadias and their son José.

Conscious of the long expanse of bare leg beneath the shabby shorts, the mud, bruises and bloodstains that marked the smooth skin, the dirty T-shirt and a face devoid of make-up, Pavane pulled herself together enough to greet the visitors charmingly, always aware of the strong pressure of Armando's fingers against her waist.

Moving across to the Cortez family, she repeated her greeting with a dignity which owed nothing to her appearance, feeling a spurt of bitter anger at the mocking appraisal of Isabella's insolent smile.

How dared Armando arrange a dinner party without

the courtesy of warning her! Just because she wasn't
responsible for the preparations it didn't mean he
should ignore her presence. In the circumstances he
deserved to be embarrassed! It was an emotion he
might not have experienced before in his adult life.
She just hoped he was smarting beneath it as much as
she was!

'I've instructed Ana to delay dinner until such time
as you are dressed to join us, *querida*.'

Did she read a threat in the seemingly gentle words?
A flicker of something that might portend revenge
showed for a moment in Armando's bright eyes,
causing her stomach to tighten nervously. It was with
a sense of resentment she accepted her dismissal,
murmuring her apologies to the assembled company
before freeing herself from his grasp and walking with
as much dignity as she could muster until she reached
the sanctuary of the house.

Once inside, she ran up the stairs, going into her
room and flinging herself down on the bed. For a
second or two she lay there trying to group her
thoughts. How could she possibly go downstairs again
and face them? Wasn't it enough that she'd already
made one exhibition of herself without compounding
the crime?

With a heavy heart she got to her feet and opened
the wardrobe, gazing in despair at its contents. There
was nothing suitable for evening wear. Certainly
nothing that wouldn't look inferior in comparison with
the beautiful dresses of the three women downstairs!
In fact only one garment lay any claims to being an
evening dress, and that had been a dreadful mistake
which should never have left England.

Unwillingly she drew it towards her. The colour
was all right—a glowing emerald green, and the silky
opalescent sheen of the material still had the same
beauty that had originally attracted her to the sale

window of an expensive boutique two years previously. Unfortunately, she had made the elementary mistake of buying without trying on. She smiled sadly, remembering how ridiculous its plunging neckline had appeared on her slim eighteen-year-old figure, and how the slit-sided skirt had displayed legs of a birdlike slimness.

How right Aunt Elaine had been when she insisted it couldn't be worn without drastic alteration. But the shawl of lace she had painstakingly applied to cover the revealing lines of the bodice hadn't quite matched, and the overall effect had been fussy and old-fashioned. She had sewn up the side split too, with the result that the skirt bunched up unattractively over her hips. What had started as a simple couture elegance had become dowdy and ridiculous!

Pavane thrust it back on its hanger, turning from the wardrobe and gasping with renewed horror as she caught sight of the mud on her face. Oh God, no wonder Armando had been ashamed of her—for hadn't that been the meaning of the still disdain on his dark face?

There was only one way out of the situation now! she would withdraw completely from the evening's entertainment. Let Isabella act as hostess to Armando. It was the role she had been destined for anyway.

Quickly Pavane pushed the intercom button on the phone and was relieved to hear Ana's pleasant voice.

'Ana, I find I've a migraine coming on. Could you please ask one of the girls to make my excuses to Don Armando and tell him I shan't be joining him and his guests for dinner. Oh, and Ana, would you go ahead with the meal without further delay?'

'Yes, of course, immediately, Doña Pavane.' Ana's voice softened, grew more personal. 'Don Armando was very worried when you and the boy were so late back. He sent Enrico and some of the men out searching for you.'

'Oh no!' That would be another black mark against her.

'I'll send Maria up to you, my dear, with something light to eat.'

Pavane had no appetite for food, but the offer was kindly meant and it was easier to accept it than give offence. She murmured her thanks before replacing the receiver. What she needed now was a long, lovely bath to ease her tired muscles.

She'd been soaking for five minutes when she heard the bedroom door open. Thinking it was Maria with the meal Ana had promised her, she was totally unprepared when the bathroom door was flung open and Armando glowered down at her.

His brilliant gaze pinned her, intimate, deliberately scathing. 'Out!' he ordered tersely, the anger in the word disturbing her equilibrium.

Pavane stared back at him, feeling the burning betraying colour rise in her face as she lifted the sponge to cover her breasts in a reflex action of modesty that made him draw his breath in with a hissing sound of irritation. The shock of his unexpected appearance had been so great she made no move to obey him. Besides, she had no wish to clamber out of the bath naked and vulnerable while he was in such a mood. But before she could protest he bent forward, his face locked into a deep scowl, and wrenched the plug from its hole.

'Out!' he thundered.

Indignant anger was mirrored on her set face as she lunged forward to replace it, only to find her upper arm firmly grasped as she was hauled to her feet.

'Here!' Armando seized the large bath towel, wrapping it round her body at underarm level, and with no thought for her dignity, looped an arm beneath her knees, lifting her clear of the bath and carrying her, too shocked to struggle, back into the bedroom.

He threw her down on to the bed with scant regard, his eyes glittering with malice as the force of his action caused her to bounce on the well-sprung mattress.

'Now, *mujer mia*,' he grated, 'get dressed and get down to your guests.'

His face was merciless, his body so taut that she shivered, yet somewhere she found the courage to defy him.

'They're not *my* guests,' she said, her voice trembling slightly despite her resolve. '*I* didn't even know they were coming. And I've no intention of going down to dinner.'

The gaze that met her wide-eyed challenge was hard and implacable. Despite her fury at the way he had handled her, Pavane could feel her pulse quickening, a kind of perverse excitement flooding her body.

'If you had returned at a reasonable hour, you would have been informed. It was a last-minute arrangement. Señor Abadias is a house guest of the Cortez. He's interested in buying some of my horses and it seemed propitious to invite him to dinner here.' He stood glaring down at her, dark brows locked in a frown over his straight, elegant nose, his mouth pressed into a determined line, his chin squared and tense. It was obvious he resented the need to explain his actions.

His voice had the cold sting of a lash as he stood over her. 'You are my wife and I demand your presence at my table!'

'Really?' Pavane clutched the towel tightly to her damp body. Knowing she was at a gross disadvantage without proper clothing, her hair in wet curls round her unmade-up face, little trickles of bath water dripping into her ears and down her cheeks, she was still determined not to be cowed by this dark, autocratic bully who had forced her into a marriage that was growing more impossible by the minute. 'And what do you propose to do if I continue to refuse—take a riding crop to me?' she taunted recklessly.

He watched her carefully, his eyes gleaming with a devilish sparkle. 'It's not a retribution that had occurred to me, *querida*,' he mocked. 'But at this moment I begin to find the idea strangely attractive!'

Was he joking? He was regarding her with a crooked smile on his mouth which fell short of his eyes. She'd been a fool to question his power to enforce obedience in a society where the demonstration of authority separated the men from the boys. She had no idea to what lengths he would go to get his own way, but she regretted putting ideas into his head which could rebound disastrously on herself.

She tried to hide her trepidation as the smile died from his lips, to be replaced with a grimness that made the short hairs on her neck rise. 'If you wish to disregard the duty your position in this house entails . . .'

'My duty as Pablo's nursemaid?' Pavane interposed with mock innocence.

Armando's steady contemplation was unnerving. 'Your duty as my wife,' he continued coolly. 'Then I'd ask you to remember that the financial security of your future rests entirely in my hands.'

Dark eyes swept comprehensively over her glowing damp body as if they could pierce the covering of the towel and see through to the soft curves of her femininity.

There was something about the gaze that mentally stripped her and brought the blood rushing to her cheeks as he continued, each word enunciated with feeling. 'And if appeals to both your ethics and your business sense fail, you might think to the preservation of your own soft skin, for I might *just* become provoked enough to treat you as the spoiled fractious child you seem determined to emulate, if you continue to oppose me!'

CHAPTER TEN

PAVANE opened her mouth to protest against Armando's threatened brutality, saw the gleam of warfare burning brightly in his eyes, and thought better of it. She knew her dirty and dishevelled appearance on the patio had shamed and irritated him and guessed he was still labouring under the throes of wanting to administer a short, sharp physical lesson to her to alleviate his own annoyance—rather in the way a man wants to kick the stone that has made him stumble and lose dignity.

Now it would be wise to exercise discretion, but stubbornly she stood by her decision. 'You'd only be ashamed of me again,' she muttered. 'I've nothing suitable to wear.'

'That's what every woman says.' His reply was cynically brief.

'Perhaps the women in your life like to pretend in these matters.' She dared to meet his cool appraisal with tempestuous eyes. 'I truly do have nothing suitable.'

'Why didn't you buy clothes with the allowance I gave you as I instructed, then?' Hands thrust into trousers' pockets, his whole attitude shouted aggression.

'Because I don't drive and I could hardly ride all the way into Seville to shop!' Damn him, she wouldn't tell him she'd been waiting for him to ask her!

'It didn't occur to you to ask Enrico to provide a driver for you? One of the men could have been spared to act as chauffeur.'

'No, it didn't occur to me,' she retorted angrily. 'Far

be it from me to disrupt the smooth running of your farm!'

Armando's mouth hardened, but otherwise he betrayed little reaction to her outburst. 'You must own something you can wear tonight,' he insisted impatiently.

The derision in his voice stung Pavane to action. Swinging her legs off the bed, she scrambled clear of it, advancing to the wardrobe, her lips tight with anger her heart beating with a hard rapid rhythm as she prepared to confront his complacency. Sliding the cupboard door open with a reckless gesture, she grabbed her wedding dress and threw it down on the bed.

'Perhaps you consider *that* suitable?' she taunted, her eyes flashing with rising fury.

'No.' His apparent calmness only added to her steadily growing temper. 'That is entirely unsuitable.'

'Good!' She was beginning to feel more sure of herself. 'I didn't want to wear this again until I walk down the aisle with the man who will be a *real* husband to me!'

Before she had time to draw another breath Armando had moved like a lithe animal of prey with economy and purpose. Pavane gave a smothered cry as she shrank back from the arrant cruelty that transformed his face, her hands rising to her face as he lifted the gown from the bed, his lean fingers embracing its softness, reaching for the vulnerable point at the base of the shaped neckline . . .

Her scream broke the silence in conjunction with the rending sound of material as he split the bodice in two parts, then with concentrated fury he ripped it cleanly from the skirt.

Bitter tears of hurt and humiliation sprang to Pavane's eyes as with deadly purpose his hands tested the strength of the skirt before tearing that into two pieces. As the tattered remains of her wedding dress were flung back to the bed, Pavane burst into a rage of passion.

'How dare you!' she spat at him. 'That was mine, mine do you hear! Melody bought it for me!'

But it wasn't the infringement of possession that had hurt so badly. She had treasured that dress, had intended to keep it all her life. Everything she had ever felt for Armando had been reflected in that dress: respect, admiration, love and desire—and a scorching, burning hatred because he hungered after her body and didn't give a damn for the aching torture of her soul!

Now he had punished what he saw as her impertinence with a cruelty more difficult to bear than any beating. If he had slapped her, her bruised skin would have healed. Nothing could repair the ruined dress, shredded in as many pieces as her own reputation.

Misery and rage mingled and exploded with an impact she couldn't control. Scarcely knowing what she was doing, she launched herself against him with the full fury of her slender body. Whimpering in distress, she pummelled at him with her fists, her fingers uncurling to claw at his chest through the fine shirt he wore.

Swearing harshly, he recoiled from her onslaught, but when he raised his arms to defend himself he used only enough power to quell her without inflicting injury. She stood trembling in his grasp, panting and breathless with spent emotion, partly ashamed, partly triumphant as she saw the angry marks of her nails on his golden skin where she had torn away his shirt.

She tried to speak, but no sound came as he lifted her once more and laid her with surprising gentleness on the bed. Too distressed even to think coherently, she buried her cheek in the pillow, uncaring what might follow.

'A wedding dress is only meant to be worn once, *amada*,' he said calmly. The soft words reached her through a haze of pain. Only Armando could make the word 'beloved' sound like an insult, she thought wearily. 'I will certainly replace its value if that is what has caused this tempest.'

There was a silence as he left her side to investigate the contents of her wardrobe, finding the emerald dress and assessing it with a critical eye. 'This will have to do.' He placed it on the bed.

So despite everything he was still insisting she should go down to dinner!

'It's awful,' she protested weakly. 'I *can't* go down in that!'

'And you can't go down as you are now,' he returned drily. 'So awful or not, it will have to do.'

Pavane shut her eyes in total wretchedness, praying she could find the words to make him relent and leave her in peace. But when he walked away it was only to go through the communicating door to his own room, returning seconds later, long fingers smoothing down the clean shirt into which he had changed.

'Armando, please . . .' She hated to beg, but she felt emotionally and physically drained. She could only disgrace him by her presence. The quality of his taste and judgment would be examined and esteemed by assessing the kind of woman he had chosen to marry. Her first impression had been disastrous. Surely her non-appearance would be preferable to her presence in the state she was in?

'Must I?' her voice wobbled alarmingly.

'Yes, I'm afraid you must.' His voice was cool and expressionless, so she must have imagined the flicker of compassion she thought she had glimpsed in the soft darkness of his eyes. 'You already have your reasons. Nothing has changed any of them. Just do your best.'

My best, she thought bitterly. What's that against the stunning beauty of Isabella or the quiet elegance of her mother or the glowing attractiveness of Señora Abadias?

'I always pay my debts . . .'

For a moment she thought it was a veiled threat, before her eyes alighted on the small parcel Armando was holding out to her. Surprised, she made no attempt to take it. Leaning across her, he placed it by her head on the pillow. 'This, you wear only for me . . .' he murmured.

For a moment she was suffocatingly aware of his nearness, the warmth of his body, the sweet smell of fresh linen, the unbearable proximity of his strong, gentle mouth. For one wild moment she thought he was going to kiss her and it was impossible to prevent the shudder of expectation that quivered through her. One kiss, one sign of encouragement, one hint that he had confidence in her and she would have faced the coming ordeal with equanimity.

It was as uncomfortable as if food had been snatched away from her mouth on the point of eating, when Armando straightened up his long frame, his cool gaze flicking a warning over her pale face.

'I shall ask Ana to organise dinner in thirty minutes.' His tone was distant. He was a man who wouldn't take 'no' for an answer, a man who intended to be obeyed. 'Be there, please, Pavane.'

It was only after she had carefully repaired the damage to her face and was satisfied her eyes no longer showed traces of her emotional storm, that Pavane had an idea.

Studying the green dress critically, remembering how attractive she had once found it, she realised how much her body had changed in the past two years. Thinness had become slimness. Her waist still had its twenty-three-inch span, but her hips and breasts had rounded, her legs developed long sweeping curves at thigh and calf.

Thoughtfully she got out her nail scissors. Whatever she did to the dress could hardly impair it! Painstakingly, aware that she was working against the clock, she cut the stitches holding the lace in place, breathing a sigh of relief as it came away cleanly leaving the deep vee neckline unmarked.

With a pang of excitement Pavane applied her scissors to the skirt, carefully snipping away where the edges of the split seam had been spliced. Satisfied at last that she had returned the dress to its original classic simplicity, she said a little prayer and stepped into it, not daring to look into the mirror until she had zipped it up and felt its welcome snugness against her body.

It was everything she had dreamed of. The cleavage was deep but not over-daring, her honey-coloured skin, soft and without blemish, glowed attractively against the sea of green, the slender sculpture of her arms looked graceful and smooth, the faint bruises from Armando's predatory fingers were hardly noticeable.

The dress fitted the smooth curve of her waist, followed the rounded line of her hips and thighs hinting at their flowing beauty, but never hugging them too tightly. High-heeled sandals made the swell of her calves more noticeable. She took a few steps, satisfying herself that the split skirt was tasteful as well as alluring.

A mounting excitement began to pulse through her. Armando had told her to do her best, and she would obey him with a vengeance! There was only one thing left to do. Curiously she opened the gift of perfume he had bought for her. Light and subtle with the barest hint of spice, it was as different as possible from the bottle he had destroyed. Thoughtfully Pavane touched it to her neck and wrists, then taking a deep breath to steady her nerves she counted to ten and went downstairs.

There was a background of music, a kaleidoscope of voices, and she heard the clock strike nine as she pushed open the door. All eyes turned towards her as she entered, but inevitably there was only one opinion that mattered.

Across the long sweep of elegant room, Armando gazed at her. If she lived to be a hundred she would never forget the look on his face. Pride, satisfaction, surprise—impossible to find just one word to describe it. Approval, yes. But more than that. Gratification? Yes, that too: but still something else. Under the warmth of his regard she felt herself flush, not questioning why her bones should turn to water, her heart beat faster as a wave of emotion flooded through her: because if she hadn't known better, she would have said Armando had looked at her with love.

Although she had been forced to attend, as the evening proceeded and dinner ended, Pavane found herself enjoying being there. Swallowing back her nervousness, she began to play the part of hostess with all the skill at her command.

At least, she thought wryly, her experience on the concert platform at college—an ordeal even embryo teachers had to face—had taught her how to disguise her nerves and to present a composed and relaxed face. From time to time her guilty eyes stole to the mark her fingernail had seared across the lean cheekbone of her husband. If anyone else noticed it, she hoped he or she would be too courteous to comment on it!

She was forced to admit to herself that her resentment at the way Armando had dared to destroy her dress was now mixed with a sense of shame at her own loss of dignity. Not only would he think she had the morals of a wildcat but the social habits too! He might have won that particular battle, she mused, but her defeat hadn't been entirely ignominious. Remembering his fury, she knew it would be a long time before she dared to confront him again in open conflict. Next time there might not be guests in the house, and heaven help her then!

To be honest, she couldn't be sure that Armando wasn't going to take her to task again after the guests had departed. She might not yet have seen the full extent of his anger—and the prospect of *that* was decidedly unsettling!

She was conscious of Isabella regarding her with a look of veiled dislike. Despite everything she had done to be pleasant to the young Spanish girl, her attempts had been met with a pointed coldness. Everyone else there had been charming—except Isabella! Still, in the circumstances it was understandable: especially if Armando had confided in her about his wife's supposed 'sins'. Resolutely she forced herself to meet Isabella's regard with fortitude. After all, the ordeal was as great for the dark-haired beauty as it was for herself. No way was she going to cast a slur on the hospitality of the Cortijo by defending herself against even one of Isabella's pointed jibes.

It was two in the morning when the Cortez family and their friends finally left. Pavane hadn't realised Armando and Isabella had remained behind the others until she heard Isabella's voice, low and furious. 'I never, ever want to set foot in your house again, or see your face, or speak to you!' she hissed. 'How dare you expect me to listen to you! I've taken just as much as I intend to! Our so-called friendship is finished, Armando—dead!'

Silently Pavane drew back into the shadows. How could she blame Isabella? What woman could be expected to put up with Armando's behaviour? It could only be hoped that Isabella would forgive him when his present marriage was dissolved. If she really loved him, she would swallow her pride.

But when she flounced out of the house a few seconds later, her face was set in a mutinous frown of temper and she walked past Pavane without a second look.

'We have to talk . . .' Armando had followed Pavane closely up the stairs, laying a halting hand on her arm as she went to turn into her bedroom.

'It's very late,' she demurred. 'Can't it wait?'

'No.' He pushed her gently into the room, closing the door behind them. 'I want to know why you changed your mind and came downstairs to dinner.'

'Really?' It was an odd question. 'I was under the impression you gave me three good reasons.'

'And I was under the impression you were going to ignore them all!' His eyebrows rose a little. 'I'm intrigued to know which of the reasons you found most persuasive.'

Suppose she told him the truth: that the maintenance of his pride before his guests was as important to her as it was to him? Instead she looked ruefully at her legs. 'I've so many bruises I hardly cared to increase their number.'

His mouth twisted wryly. 'They were words spoken in the heat of the moment. I could never hurt you.'

She thought of the wedding dress, lying in pieces at the bottom of the wardrobe, and made no reply.

He glanced at her quizzically. 'If only it had been one of the other reasons.'

'You prefer to think me dutiful or mercenary rather than a coward?' She sent him an amazed smile. 'Does it matter? After all, you got your own way.'

She watched with curious eyes as he walked across to the door leading to the balcony, flinging it open so the warm night air filled the room, before turning to face her again. 'I'd hoped to use the same reason to persuade you to spend the rest of your life here,' he said simply. Then, reading in her face some of the confusion she was feeling, he added quietly, 'I've no wish to end this marriage, Pavane, neither do I wish to maintain it in its present state.'

A quiver of apprehension raced through her as her breathing quickened beneath his enigmatic gaze. Lost for words, she could only shake her head.

'Do you understand me?' he asked gravely. 'I want to turn this farce into a real productive relationship.'

Without even stopping to consider what he might mean by 'productive' she knew there could only be one answer. 'No!' The word burst from horror-stricken lips. 'I mean, it's not what we agreed—what you promised me!'

'Then you must release me from that promise.'

Pavane stared at him distrustfully, shaking her head in bewilderment. It must be Isabella's rejection that had caused him to act like this, a burning desire to revenge himself on his beautiful compatriot. Somehow she had to find the words to refuse him, but her mouth was dry and her throat restricted.

'It would make good sense for both of us ...' Armando walked round to stand in front of her, taking her hands into his own. 'Listen, Pavane ...' His face was intent, drawn even, as she raised frightened eyes to meet his sombre regard. 'I've heard from Ramón. He's been offered a partnership in a business in Brazil and he's decided to accept it.'

'And Dolores?' For a moment her own quandary was forgotten.

He gave a short ironic laugh. 'Dolores has agreed to stay with him. It seems he took the decision without consulting her, and his display of authority impressed her.' His mouth curled derisively. 'Dolores has always respected a man who is prepared to dominate her. That's been one of Ramón's problems. He loves her too much to disregard her arguments and she takes his tolerance as weakness. In this instant he acted for himself, and it seems to have reaped dividends.'

'I'm glad,' Pavane told him sincerely.

'Yes, so am I.' His hands still held hers, his thumbs rubbing gently, almost hypnotically against her palms. 'It means, of course, they want Pablo to go to South America with them.'

'Of course . . .' Pavane felt the blood seep from her face. She had been too pleased to think about the mended marriage to consider its implications for Armando. He would have wanted his heir to grow up in Spain knowing and loving the Cortijo as he did. With Perico years away from marriage and Isabella apparently lost to him, it was clear why Armando had changed his mind about his own marriage.

He was watching the expressions chase across her open face, smiling with a grim humour as he read her mind. 'It was you who told me I should have sons,' he reminded her.

'Yes.' She was conscious of fluttering sensations erupting in her stomach beneath those darkly amused eyes. 'And *you* who told *me* you didn't believe children should be born for the sole purpose of inheriting property.'

'Ah, but then ours wouldn't be, *querida*.' Slowly his eyes travelled over her body and she felt herself glow with an inner heat. His words burned into her brain, making her senses leap and her heart thump with a violence that made her tremble. Armando was watching her carefully, dark eyes mirroring his intensity, his fast shallow breathing a witness to his own agitation.

Everything within her cried out to accept what he was offering. However short it fell of the ideal fantasy of love she had nurtured since she was a child, it was what she wanted: but it was impossible—and she couldn't tell him why!

A flush compounded of misery and embarrassment swept over her as she stiffened in his embrace, trying to push him away.

'Listen to me, Pavane,' he told her harshly, his arms repossessing her, their grasp stronger. 'What have you got to lose? You've no other home, your sister will be your closest neighbour, you may have whatever you want within reason. If you want to travel, then we will. If you want to take up your music again, then you can. We'll go to Madrid and buy the best piano in Spain . . . I'll arrange private tuition for you . . .' His voice thickened as she flinched beneath the urgent movement of his fingers. 'Do you understand what I'm saying? I'm asking you to name your price!'

Bleak dismay allied to a dangerous excitement rushed through her, linked to a premonition that the situation was beyond her power to handle. Armando was playing the part of supplicant, but for how much longer would he accept that humble role? Pavane didn't need to look at his set face to be aware of the tension building in his strong body.

Never in her life had she been so totally encompassed by the dominating power, the aggression that was the core of his masculinity. For the moment Armando was pleading with her, but in the eyes of the law and the Church it was a courtesy to which she wasn't entitled.

'I—I have no price,' she faltered. Unknowingly her eyes beseeched his mercy. 'I'm not for sale.'

'No.' An unexpected gentleness smoothed his features as a smile trembled on his mouth. 'No, my love, I never really expected you were.' She stood bewitched as he touched her face with the gentle tribute of a connoisseur of loveliness. 'What you give, you give freely out of joy and without a thought of consequence.'

'Armando . . .' Her voice was scarcely audible, her

throat parched with the fear his remark had aroused.
He was reminding her that in his eyes she was no
better than a *puta* unworthy of respect or consideration.

Slowly, as if he was afraid of frightening her
further, his hand drifted down to push first one then
the other thin strap away from her shoulders. There
was nothing she could do to stop him or to control the
mounting surge of emotions that shivered through her,
not least of which, she recognised with a sick dread,
was a growing need to abandon herself to him utterly:
to offer her body, heart and spirit to the man who held
her against his thundering heart, whose mouth traced
a passage of liquid fire from her shoulder towards the
deep valley between her breasts.

'Why not to me, then, *adorada mia*?' He murmured
the question against the growing heat of her skin.
'Why not give yourself to me, hmm?' His mouth
pursued a teasing journey to her mouth, touching her
parted lips so briefly that its passing caress awakened
an urgent hunger for its return.

With every fibre of his being he was willing her to
accept his proposal. She could feel the sheer force of
his personality reaching out to her, weakening her
resolve, dulling her wits, making her forget all the
reasons she dared not let him love her. She was being
swamped by the magic of a charisma that was turning
her bones to jelly, her blood to water. In her earlier
innocence she had believed she could fight Armando.
Now her own body was betraying her, and the battle
was lost.

Closing her eyes, Pavane moaned aloud, feeling her
strength draining from her. A deep sob begged his
compassion as, unable to speak the words, she pleaded
silently to ensure her own preservation.

'*Madre de Dios!*' The words were torn huskily and
broken from his ardent mouth. Whatever he had read

on her face had been enough to arouse the prowling male animal uppermost in him. Before she could move or even think his firm, beautiful mouth had taken her own in an act of erotic intimate possession and she had raised her hands to his head, touching the crisp black hair, encouraging and increasing the penetrating ardour of his kiss.

Overwhelmed by the burning flame that scorched his body and laid its white-hot power upon her, Pavane lay dormant in Armando's arms as his hands travelled down the silky fabric of her dress, drawing her into himself, making her urgently aware of his mounting desire. Finding the zip fastener, his eager fingers released it. Holding her momentarily away from himself he drew the emerald sheath down her body, seizing her close to lift her free before placing her on the bed, where she lay gasping, her senses clamouring for his return.

When he did, he had torn off his shirt, and she shivered with mounting excitement as the naked flesh of his chest touched her own. She made no protest, just a little cry of expectation as he slid her half-slip down, his hands returning to stroke her thighs, to nourish the trickle of desire until it became a hot flood of longing singing through her blood. Ripe for his love, her judgment held in frozen suspension beneath the sensual attack to which he had subjected her, Pavane was ready to receive him unconditionally. If he had moved then; if he had trapped her with his hard muscled legs; if he had simply taken what she no longer defended, she would have been a willing victim. Instead she felt his lips slowly and reluctantly relinquish the aching bud of the breast they had been cherishing.

'Pavane, *mi amor* . . .' His voice was thick and slurred—or was it just the pounding of her own blood in her ears that seemed to distort it? She stared mistily

with passion-drugged eyes at his beloved face. 'Pavane
. . .' She couldn't raise her eyes from the slow perfect
curves of his mouth, warmed and slightly swollen by
her own desperate response to his kisses. 'Tell me you
want me . . . let me hear you say it . . .' The voice that
breathed through those vulnerable lips now twisting in
a mixture of physical and mental agony, was half
strangled by effort. Mindlessly she stared at him,
hearing but not understanding. '*Dios!* Don't you see!
We're going to be bound for life . . . I have to know
it's what you want too!'

Pictures flashed through her mind in rapid
succession. Skin to skin, heart to heart, limbs
intertwined, poised trembling above an abyss of
sensual pleasure, there was no way she could prevent
the stream of memories flashing past. Melody's face
ravaged with terror; Rodrigo's uplifted arm holding
the riding crop, his face snarled with bitter fury;
Perico's young face, bruised and broken . . . then the
joy, the open adoration as Melody and Rodrigo
exchanged glances on her wedding day. She had taken
it upon herself to save her sister's marriage. What
right had she to plunge it into jeopardy for her own
selfish gratification?

She moaned inarticulately, her body moving
spasmodically beneath him. Armando possessed a
fierce, autocratic pride, and for him to discover he had
been duped into a marriage which had resulted in
Isabella deserting him would be to invite a cruel and
swift retaliation.

'Pavane!' He had sensed without comprehending
her torment. The roughness of his voice echoed her
own anguish. 'One word, just one word, *amada mia*
. . . just "yes"!'

His laboured breathing filled her ears. She could
feel the tremor of his body beneath her fingers, his
sweet warm breath on her cheek.

It took every positive power of her mind to overcome the melting lethargy of her body, but she managed it. 'No,' she whispered. Then as she felt him freeze in disbelief, her voice strengthened, her hands pushed vainly at his chest in an attempt to dislodge his commanding weight from her supple form. 'No, Armando, I can't. Not with you. Not ever with you!'

She never knew precisely when he left. She only knew by the time she had gained some control over herself, he had gone silently and soundlessly, leaving her to enjoy the hell she had made for herself.

CHAPTER ELEVEN

'MELODY!'

Pavane clutched the phone closer to her ear as her sister's voice, bubbling with happiness, came over the line. 'How are you both?'

Over a week had passed since she had rejected Armando—a week where he had treated her with a coolness that was eating into her soul. Yet how could she blame him? Unable to explain her motive, she could only endure his indifference in silence.

How often during that time had she longed for the solace of her sister's company. If only she could have been certain Melody and Rodrigo were happy, that her sacrifice hadn't been in vain! The phone call was an answer to her prayer.

'Oh, Pavvy darling, you'll never guess!' Melody's voice was edged with a shrill excitement. 'I think I'm going to have a baby. Of course it's early days yet, but all the signs are there and I just feel I'm right!'

'That's fantastic!' Pavane swallowed the lump in her throat. 'I'm so happy for you.'

'How about you?' There was real concern in Melody's question. 'Are you all right, Pavvy? I keep thinking about you and Armando. Is he treating you well?'

'Yes, of course.' What else could she say? 'He—he . . .' Horrified, she found herself beginning to cry.

'Pavvy, what is it? What's wrong? Oh, my God, what's he done to you?'

'Nothing, Melly,' she hastened to reassure her sister. 'It's just that you were right about him not being made of wood . . .' She hadn't meant to tell

Melody, but the temptation to confide in someone was overwhelming, and who else was there who would understand?

'Oh, dear Lord!' There was an appalled silence before Melody continued. 'Did he . . . has he . . .'

'He asked me to forget about getting the marriage dissolved, that's all. He—he didn't touch me.'

'What did you say? What happened?'

'What could I say?' Pavane gave a desperate little laugh. 'If we made love he'd know I'd lied to him about Perico. He'd discover I've never been loved by any man.'

'But you wanted to say yes? You've fallen in love with him, Pavane?' Melody homed in accurately to the truth.

'I . . .' Oh, what was the point of lying? She'd never been able to keep a secret from Melody. 'Yes, I love him, Melly, but I won't let you down, I promise you. And Armando won't force me. He's accepted the fact that I don't want to stay married to him.'

There was a few moments' silence while Pavane fought to stop her tears, then Melody spoke again, her voice low and thoughtful. 'I've taken too much from you already, my love. I'm not selfish enough to take any more. You gave me the chance to keep the man I love. I want to give you the same chance. If you love Armando, give yourself to him.'

'But Melly . . .' protested Pavane, a wild hope surging in her, 'when he finds out he'll hate us both for the way we've lied to him!'

Melody sighed. 'He may never find out, Pavvy. A man can't always tell if a girl is a virgin or not. It's not always obvious, especially in the passion of the moment. Believe me, he may never know he was the first.'

'But if he does?' There was an element of truth in what Melody had told her. Somewhere she had read that in as many as fifty per cent of women their virginity was indetectable. Could she take that chance?

'Then I'll have to throw myself on his mercy.' Melody gave a wry laugh. 'If he loves you, you'll have to intercede on my behalf.'

How could Pavane explain to her sister that love didn't come into the picture as far as Armando was concerned and any plea for clemency would fall on deaf ears? No, the whole situation was impossible.

'Pavane—are you still there?'

'Yes, yes, of course. But I can't risk it, Melody. I won't prejudice your happiness, especially now if you're going to have a baby.'

'And I won't prejudice yours any longer, Pavane!' There was a strength in Melody's voice that surprised her. 'I've taken too much from you already. If I hadn't been so self-centred and weak in the beginning you would never have been in this mess. These past weeks with Rodrigo have been so wonderful and I've been so happy I feel I can face up to anything now.'

'And risk losing everything?' Pavane was tossing aside her own happiness with every word, but what alternative was there?

'It's a risk I've got to take If I'm going to be able to live with myself, Pavvy. Think about it. If it's what you really want, then take the chance. At least that way there's a fifty-fifty chance he'll never guess what happened. Otherwise . . .' Pavane could actually hear the deep intake of breath the other end, 'otherwise I'll have no chance at all, because I shall go to Armando myself as soon as we return and tell him exactly what happened!'

'Melody—no!' Truly aghast, Pavane sought her mind for fresh argument, but it was too late. The line had gone dead.

★   ★   ★

What the brass band lacked in skill it compensated for in volume. Against the ageless whitewashed houses of Campos Altos with their grilled windows and balconies hung with flowers, their green shutters peeling beneath the scorching caress of the mid-morning sun, the brash performance of modern pop music seemed strangely incongruous. Yet Pavane knew the mixture of old culture and contemporary innovation was typical of modern Spain.

She gazed around the central square of the village, transformed by stalls and sideshows, balloon sellers and popcorn kiosks. Really she had had no wish to attend the *feria* at all, especially after the unsettling conversation she'd had with Melody earlier that morning. She had needed to go somewhere quiet and really think out the consequences of what she did next. Last time she had dived into a pool of intrigue totally unaware of how deep the waters would prove for her. It was a mistake she didn't want to make a second time! In the event, Pablo's excitement had been so overwhelming, she had agreed to let Enrico drive them both in from the Cortijo an hour earlier. Everywhere people were laughing and talking or taking refreshment at one of the many sprawling outdoor cafés that had extended their seating capacity in honour of the annual fair. The atmosphere was buoyant with excitement. She was, Pavane thought miserably, probably the unhappiest person there.

Her mind still a mass of jumbled, troubled thoughts, she wandered over towards the church, stepping across its cool threshold. Had she been too arrogant in daring to assume responsibility for Melody's actions? If so, she was paying a just penalty for her interference; suffering the agony Melody had wished she might never know—of loving and wanting without hope of fulfilment.

She walked slowly towards the altar, drawn once

more to gaze at the olive wood statue. A slight noise behind her made her turn, to see Enrico's mother regarding her with interest from one of the front pews.

'You've come to admire my lovely Elena?' she asked, continuing before Pavane could reply. 'Beautiful, isn't she, and how proud she would have been if she'd lived long enough to see it finished . . .'

'Elena?' Had Miguel de Montilla's mistress and his wife shared the same name? Pavane looked closely at the old lady, remembering Enrico had told her his mother used to work at the Cortijo. She, of all people, could probably identify the subject of the carving.

'Elena de Montilla—Miguel's wife, of course! Who else would it be? He was devoted to her. The day she died, he took his young son Ignacio—still a toddler— and disappeared for months, heartbroken.' Enrico's mother rocked backwards and forwards, hugging her arms across her body. 'As if I would ever forget the day! It was the first time I had heard a grown man cry aloud in his pain.'

'But Elena was disfigured—ugly . . .' Perplexed, Pavane was sure the old lady had made some mistake.

'Disfigured, yes! But ugly—never. One side of her poor face was marked as black as a ripe damson—but the other—Dios! She was exquisite!' Her shrewd eyes narrowed in her wrinkled face. 'Why else would Miguel give up the pencil and the brush to take up the knife? It was the one way he could do his wife justice. In olive wood there is no colour, no stain to mar the beauty of bone and flesh. He carved Elena as he had always seen her—as beautiful as the dawn.' She stared searchingly at Pavane. 'You think I'm mad? That I don't know? Heavens, girl, I was her maid—I knew her face as well as my own.'

The likeness was there! Pavane had been blind not to see it before. Their grandmother's blood had influenced the striking handsomeness of the Montilla men. 'But Armando himself has no idea it's Elena de Montilla!' she protested excitedly as her delight at the discovery overcame her previous sadness.

'Why should he?' Enrico's mother shrugged. 'He wasn't even born here. Why should it matter to him anyway? It all happened a long, long time ago.'

But of course it mattered. Miguel de Montilla was his grandfather. Armando shared his name and his blood, and what he had seen as a public slight to his grandmother had cut deeply and painfully. Yet all the time the truth had been there in front of his eyes, and a live witness to Miguel's integrity had actually been living on his own land.

Outside the clarion call of a trumpet disturbed the peace, drawing Pavane's attention as the old lady settled more comfortably in her seat. 'Go on, my dear, the *desfile* is just about to start, you won't want to miss that. I shall stay here and rest.'

Obediently Pavane left the church, still elated with her discovery, and returned to the square.

Pablo had told her about the *Desfile des Señores*. The procession that was the key part of the *feria*. Emulating the customs of the past when local grandes—the lords of Cordoba—had deigned to ride through the village, the local landowners and dignitaries paraded through the square and down the narrow streets on horseback, while the villagers cheered and the children darted between the riders in a daring game of nerve and skill.

Now, entering the square before her, Pavane could see about a dozen horses and riders dressed in traditional Andalusian style wearing the *traje corte*— the suit of tight trousers and short jacket, the wide-brimmed Cordoban hat worn straight on heads held arrogantly high. It was a scene of beauty and elegance as the horsemen showed off their expert skills. But Pavane had eyes for only one.

Armando sat astride a white stallion: ramrod-stiff in the saddle, his long, tightly muscled legs elegantly clad in the slim-cut trousers shown to advantage by the long-stirruped riding fashion of the region. His right hand rested on his thigh, the thumb following the line of his groin, fingers splayed backwards across the tautly stretched material clothing the lean outline of his hip.

He held the reins gathered loosely in his left hand away from his body at chest height. Beneath the straight-brimmed hat, his profile was still and remote as if it, too, had been carved from the olive wood so beloved by Miguel.

'*El es mucho hombre, no?*' The softly worded question whispered in a man's amused voice close to her ear brought a cry of surprise to Pavane's lips as, turning abruptly, she came face to face with Perico.

'*Por Dios!*' she cried out. 'What are *you* doing here?' Anxiously her eyes sought Armando's retreating back.

Perico grinned. 'What a way to greet your brother-in-law! I've come to see the *feria*, of course, and watch my beloved brother play lord of the manor.' There was amused affection in his pleasant voice. 'He does it with style, doesn't he?'

'I'm sorry, Perry,' Pavane apologised for the lack of warmth in her greeting, but the emotional atmosphere at the Cortijo was strained enough without Perico defying his brother's instructions. She had sensed the violence simmering beneath the controlled surface of Armando's behaviour. It only needed a simple goad to prick the bubble of civilisation and reveal the savage beneath it. She was desperately afraid that Perry's arrival might provide just such a stimulus. 'It's just that I didn't expect to see you.'

'There's no need to look so stricken.' He eyed her curiously, a good-looking young man casually dressed in jeans and T-shirt, an age away from the saturnine figure, controlling the power of the white stallion with his hands and heels, bringing it to its hind legs to stand pawing the air while daring children ran beneath its flailing hooves. 'Didn't Armando tell you the prodigal has been invited home? The errant brother forgiven and welcomed back to the fold?'

'No.' The monosyllable issued from dry lips as she searched his face hoping for further explanation. 'No, Armando has said nothing to me.'

Perico grinned wryly. 'Perhaps he intended it as a pleasant surprise!' His dark eyes devoured her face and for the first time she saw caution mirrored in their depths. 'Pavane, forgive me—I really did love Melody, you know, although that's no excuse for the way I treated her.' For the first time she saw the signs of strain on his face. 'These last weeks have been hellish for me, wondering if she was all right, what was happening to her . . .'

Pavane answered the unspoken question. 'I spoke to her today. She thinks she may be going to have a baby.'

He tried to smile, but she had seen the pain arrow across his eyes. 'That's good news.'

A warm smile softened her face, as she realised she and Perry had something in common apart from their shared deception of Armando and Rodrigo. Both of them were lovesick and heart-torn. With a spontaneous gesture of friendship she placed her hand on his arm. 'I'm so glad Armando's decided to forget the past and welcome you back here.'

'Thank you, Pavvy.' There was real warmth in his answering smile. 'It's great to know you've forgiven me. It's good to come home.'

Neither of them saw the white stallion prance past or glimpsed the lines of pain etched on the harsh profile of its rider.

*   *   *

Perry was laughing at some juvenile joke of his nephew's while Pavane stared sightlessly at the glass of wine he had persuaded her to have, when Armando arrived at their table. He had dismounted on the farther side of the square, walking with a lazy elegant stride through the crowds that milled in its centre. If he had looked a superb specimen of manhood mounted on the white stallion, then his appearance was in no way diminished now he was on foot.

The short jacket emphasised his broad shoulders and lean muscled waist: the narrow trousers fitted smooth as a snakeskin across his flat abdomen, flattering the long sweeping curves of his thighs and calves above the elegant riding boots.

'Armando.' Perry rose from the table, his movement supple and relaxed, but his eyes wary. It was clear he was uncertain of his reception.

'Rico.' Armando greeted him civilly, but coolly with a sharp downward flick of his head, at the same time placing a hand on the younger man's shoulder indicating he should sit down again.

'Can you take me with you on your horse, Tio?' Pablo demanded eagerly. 'Can you take me for a ride round the square before we eat?'

'I'm sorry.' Armando smiled at the boy, a swift sad movement of his lips totally without humour. 'I'm afraid I won't be having lunch with you. That's what I've come to tell you. Unexpectedly, I find I have to attend a meeting in Seville.'

'But surely you can eat first?' Pavane spoke impulsively, unable to hide her disappointment.

'I'm afraid not.' For the first time he looked at her, and she flinched before the emptiness of those brilliant eyes. Perhaps it was the effect of his suit, perhaps it was Perry's presence, but she had never felt so much of a stranger in an alien culture as she did at that moment. 'I intend to ride straight back to the Cortijo. Ana can get me a snack while I change, then I'll drive myself up.'

'But you'll miss the fireworks tonight!' Such a disaster was beyond Pablo's comprehension. 'Must you go?'

'I'm afraid so.' Armando's voice softened noticeably as he addressed his nephew. 'Don't worry, *you* won't miss them. Your uncle and aunt will make sure you have a good time.' The bright brown eyes became a positive dynamic force in the stillness of his lean face, gleaming now with an aching awareness behind the shadow of his thick, dark lashes as they came to rest on his brother. 'You'll look after Pavane for me, won't you, Rico? She hasn't lived here long enough to know all our customs. She needs a guide and a friend.'

Somewhere in her heart a dagger twisted. I need *you*! she wanted to call out in her anguish. Biting her lip, she looked down at her tensely locked fingers.

'I'll be honoured to escort your wife.'

Pavane watched Armando's lips twist with cynical amusement at the stiff formality of his brother's reply, but he contented himself with a nod of acknowledgement, as sliding his hand into his pocket he withdrew a slender leather wallet and laid it on the table. 'Naturally, I shall still be your host,' he murmured smoothly.

He turned as if to go, then paused. 'By the way, *querida*,' Pavane tensed beneath his sombre gaze, a feeling of deep apprehension flooding through her veins at the sardonic use of the word 'darling', 'it looks as if this meeting will be a long one, culminating in dinner, so rather than drive back in the early hours, I've booked a room for the night.'

'Oh!' She couldn't think of anything else to say, her bewilderment plain to see in the innocent lift of her eyes as she fought for an understanding of his behaviour. Lazily, Armando moved to stand beside her chair, lifting one of her hands away from her lap and raising it to his mouth in a gesture of old-time courtesy that matched his dignified and elegant appearance.

Lightly, his lips brushed her soft skin as they had at that first meeting. Since that moment they had taken their toll from nearly every satin inch of her body. Pavane shuddered, a deep uncontrollable spasm traversing her from head to toe.

She heard the hiss of breath between his teeth before he released her hand as if its touch burnt him. Then he was striding away, the crowds parting before his purposeful approach. Head held high, he seemed to tower above the villagers, his lean-hipped stride eating up the distance to where the white stallion stood restlessly pawing the ground, awaiting its master.

Pavane slept fitfully, her mind filled with images of Armando. She was dreaming of watching him in the arms of some beautiful Sevillan girl, his body crushed against hers, his mouth taking violent possession of scarlet lips, his strong body subduing a pliant form that offered only token resistance the more to inflame him into demanding complete submission. For hadn't that been the reason for Armando's sudden departure? The first sign he had forsaken any hope of getting her to change her mind? A gesture made publicly and pointedly in front of his brother as an indication that all wasn't well between them? Now, when she was nerving herself to risk everything to hold him—wasn't he showing her it was already too late!

She was awakened suddenly, her heart pounding fiercely, the blood drumming against her ears, her body convulsed in powerful trembling. She shot bolt upright. Something had disturbed the stillness of the night, causing her abrupt return to consciousness—but what?

As her eyes grew used to the dim, moonlit room she could make out the hands of her small alarm clock—four in the morning! She took a deep controlled breath, that was the surest way of helping her heart resume its normal beat. Then she heard footsteps crossing the patio. Should she ring down to where the servants slept? She hesitated; whoever was walking towards the house was making no attempt to be silent. It was probably Perico. She had left the two young men to follow their own devices after they had escorted Pablo and herself back to the Cortijo shortly after midnight. At that time the arrangement had been that Perico would go back to the *hacienda* with Esteban and spend the rest of the night there, but he could easily have changed his mind.

When, after a few more minutes, she heard the front door open, then close, she relaxed. The movements were so deliberate it couldn't be a burglar—it must be Perico! She listened to the steady footsteps mounting the stairs, heard them pass her door and fade away down the corridor to where Perico's room had been prepared.

Sighing a deep sigh of relief, she stretched languorously and turned to plump up her pillow. Seconds later her body tensed. The footsteps were returning! Frowning, she listened, hearing them come to a halt outside her door, followed by a sharp rap on the wood. Switching on the dim bedside light, she went to the door, preparing to open it slightly, totally unprepared for the sudden thrust from outside that sent her reeling backwards into the room.

Armando stood there like an avenging angel, raw fury blazing from his eyes. Clipped and savage, his words ripped into the silent fabric of the night. 'Perico's not in his room, and his bed hasn't been slept in!'

CHAPTER TWELVE

SHOCK, anger and a burning resentment: Pavane experienced all three as Armando strode into the room, kicking the door closed behind him.

'So you assumed he was sharing mine?' At a total disadvantage, her hair tousled, her eyes still drowsy with sleep, her thin nightdress doing little to conceal the warm curves of the naked body beneath it, Pavane faced the scalding ferocity of his gaze with an icy calm.

So this was what he had planned all the time! To pretend to stay away for the night in order to catch Perico and herself playing the part of lovers!

'I thought it was possible, yes.' There was no triumph in the dark, heavy-lidded eyes, only a terrible weariness. Yet his physical presence dominated the room—a vibrant, accusing force.

Rigid with pain, Pavane thrust her small chin at him challengingly. 'Perhaps you'd like to search my wardrobe? Or go through into your own room and look for him there?' she flung at him.

'You don't understand . . .' There was a catch in his voice that brought her attention sharply to his face.

'There isn't much to understand, is there?' Her tone was scathing but her heart was beating uncontrollably again, waves of despair making her body tremble. 'If I'd known you wanted to come in and find me in bed with your brother, I'd have begged him to stay—rather than to spend the night with Esteban at the *hacienda*.'

'It wasn't like that . . .'

A growing awareness was running through Pavane's nerves, shocking her into vibrant alertness. It took all

174

her strength not to reach out to him and touch the
beads of sweat that stood out on his top lip.

'The last thing I wanted was to find you together!'

'No?' Her voice trembled. Dear God, if she only
dared believe him! 'Then why tell me you were
spending the night in Seville?'

'Because I intended to.' Armando stared down into
her face. Uneasily she returned his fervid appraisal. 'I
meant to leave you and Perico together for a whole
day,' he continued, keeping his voice level with a
perceptible effort. 'A day in which you would be free
of my presence, my influence, to discover for
yourselves if you still loved each other . . . still wanted
each other . . .' A curious sense of unreality pervaded
Pavane, keeping her silent before the evidence of his
tortuous reasoning. '*Madre de Dios!*—can't you see? I
separated you for my own selfish reasons. I've told
you, the moment I saw you in church, I was
bewitched by you. The sweet poison of your eyes
inflamed me beyond sanity! I couldn't even think
straight.' He laughed harshly. 'The first time I saw
you I was entranced. You were my brother's *novia*—
but that didn't matter. I would challenge him for you:
fairly if possible, unfairly if necessary!' The hand that
reached out and took her chin was gentle, but she had
made no effort to escape it anyway. Armando lifted
her face towards him, staring down with a glinting
intensity into her puzzled eyes. 'What do you think I
felt that night when Rodrigo delivered Rico to me,
beaten up and smelling of your perfume, and flung
him at my feet with the demand that he should marry
you forthwith because he'd dishonoured you? Well,
querida . . .' He gave her a beautiful cruel smile, then
before she was aware of his intention he lowered his
head and kissed her with a leashed passion that
terrified her. 'What do you think that did to me,
hmm?'

The sudden ruthlessness of his voice made her shiver. Wordlessly she shook her head, conscious of the warmly throbbing tissue of her lips.

'There was no way I could hand you over to my brother at that moment. I'm a man, not a saint, and I knew there was no way I could live with you as my sister-in-law.' He laughed bitterly. 'We're told that Hell is to be deprived of the sight of God. Not so. Hell to me is being made to live with something you desire, but cannot possess!'

He walked away towards the bed, hands thrust into his pockets, shoulders hunched. Deep within herself Pavane felt a tenuous growing hope begin to root, nourished by the astounding depths of passion in his deep voice.

As he spun round to face her again the strange mingling of pride and pain on his dark countenance lent an increased drama to his words. 'I could have paid for you to return to England—but what sort of purgatory would that have sentenced me to? So I talked you into marriage. Persuaded you I didn't want you, when all the time I could think of nothing but possessing you, feeling your body beneath mine . . . loving you . . .' He moved restlessly as Pavane felt her body respond to his words as if they had been caresses. Instinctively her hands rose to touch her own aching breasts.

'I thought you needed time.' The huskiness of that dark male voice was a seduction in itself. 'Time to forget Perico. I told myself he was young and ardent but fickle. He wasn't what you really wanted or needed and in time you would realise it. Yes, I was arrogant!' He smiled grimly, picking up her unspoken reaction. 'And I was a blind fool too. I thought I could leave you alone long enough to get over Rico naturally. *Dios*, Pavane! I'd never felt for any woman the way I feel for you.

'Perhaps it was that, perhaps it was because we were truly man and wife, perhaps it was because I found you in Rico's arms on our wedding day—but I couldn't keep away from you that night. I was on fire for you, and when I felt your body respond to mine I would have broken every promise I'd made to you without shame or regret . . .' He paused, thumping one fist hard into the palm of his other hand, his breathing heavy, his voice thick with emotion.

'Armando . . .' whispered Pavane, her body warm with the memory of how her flesh had quickened to his touch.

'Until I smelled your perfume, the same perfume that had been on my brother's body, on his hair, and I knew it was Rico you wanted, Rico your body begged for—not me.' He swallowed with visible effort as his tortured eyes swept across her stricken face. 'And then you cried out that you loved me . . . and I knew it was Perico you called to . . .'

'No, oh no!' Pavane's voice broke on a sob.

'God knows,' Armando ignored her outburst, making no pains to hide the anguish that had forced white lines each side of his tender mouth, 'I couldn't take you. Not like that.' His face twisted into a travesty of a smile. 'If I'd only wanted the satisfaction of your body it might have been all right, but you see, *querida*. I'd begun to love you . . .'

'Love?' Wide-eyed, she repeated the word, hardly able to credit it. 'But you loved Isabella. You were going to marry her until your hand was forced.'

'Marry Isabella?' He looked astounded, his dark brows clashing on his smooth forehead. 'In the name of God, who told you such nonsense?'

'I—I . . .' she stammered, unwilling to implicate Ana. 'You told Dolores and Ramón you were going to announce your engagement—and that was before you'd even met me!'

'Oh, that!' Armando made an impatient movement with his shoulders. 'I've already told you Dolores is the type of woman who needs a masterful man to satisfy her, and Ramón is too considerate. We both knew her when we were young, but there was never anything between Dolores and myself except mutual antipathy! But she would use any weapon to needle Ramón, and she had begun to taunt him with the fact that I was still unmarried, hinting that I held a deathless passion for her. I wasn't going to let him go away to try for a reconciliation with Dolores spouting that kind of poison to hurt him. So,' he met her gaze without flinching, 'yes I told them I had plans for marriage. I certainly didn't mention a name—because there wasn't one!'

'Oh!' Pavane was totally astounded. 'But—but the other night, you and Isabella quarrelled. I thought it was because she wasn't prepared to wait any longer for you to get rid of me.'

'We quarrelled all right.' Armando's tone was grim. 'She presumed too much on our friendship when she took it on herself to treat you with less than common courtesy. Do you suppose I didn't notice her attitude that evening? It was appalling, and I told her as much.'

Pavane took a deep breath, trying to control the painful tightening of her diaphragm, the singing noise of her own blood pulsating rapidly against her eardrums. He didn't love Isabella—and what else had he said?

Slowly she walked to the bed, and sat down on it, raising beseeching blue eyes to his saturnine face, her heart leaping with a fierce joy as she drank in every curve and hollow of his proud profile.

'You said you'd begun to—to love me?' The words were scarcely more than a whisper, as if to speak them too loudly would destroy them.

'Yes. Yes, I loved you, Pavane.' The tormented eyes that met her gaze reinforced the meaning of his words. 'I began to see how cruel I'd been to you, tearing you away from Rico, never giving your love for each other a chance. I was torn between wanting you with a desperation that was burning me up, and a fear that if I took advantage of your feelings for my brother and your loneliness and the false position I'd manoeuvred you into, in the cold light of morning you'd hate me with an intensity that would make the marriage I'd forced you into a living hell for both of us!' He swallowed with visible difficulty as Pavane searched her astounded mind to find the right thing to say, speaking again before her numbed intelligence had come to her aid. 'So I compelled myself to leave you alone and suffered the tortures of the damned, night after night, pacing up and down the patio listening to the melodies that drifted from your bedroom: sad and eloquent, passionate and throbbing with longing, they told me the secrets of your heart more clearly than if you'd spoken them aloud to me!'

He paused, staring down at the floor, and she could see the effort his confession was costing him. Dear heaven! He had heard and understood her subconscious plea to be loved, but he had mistakenly thought it was Rico she wanted! Somehow she must disillusion him, wipe away the pain that had turned his face into a mask. But again he forestalled her.

'So I sent for Rico because I couldn't bear to see you suffer any more. I meant to come back in the morning, but I couldn't sleep, couldn't think, couldn't bear waiting any longer. If you and Rico still wanted each other I told myself I wouldn't stand in your way. Whatever the difficulties they could be overcome with effort and money. But I had to know the truth. Believe me,' he looked at her pale face and she flinched away from the naked pain in the depth of his compelling eyes, 'the last thing I wanted was to find you together. I went straight to Perico's room to demand the truth from him . . . and found it empty.'

'So you thought he was with me?' Pavane's voice was tender as she responded to his anguish.

'Or that you'd gone away together,' he agreed tonelessly. 'The thing is . . .' slowly he came towards her, sitting on the bed and taking her unresisting body into his arms, 'I can't let him have you! I won't let you go!'

His grip tightened as he crushed her mouth with his own, parting her lips with a desperate passion. She shivered beneath the sensual assault, the total ravishment of her mouth, but it was a shiver of excitement rather than fear. This time there would be no turning back. Melody had absolved her from the consequences that acknowledging her love for Armando might bring. Whatever the future held, this night Armando should know the real depth of her feelings for him. So when he pushed her down on the bed with the weight of his own body she made no effort to resist him. Instead with a murmur of pleasure she pressed herself seductively against him, triumphantly aware of the hardening male contours of his body.

'Pavane?' Sensing her compliance, Armando whispered her name in a soft, thick voice. She stirred languidly as his mouth followed the line of her cheek, flirted with her mouth, nibbled at her, caressed her with a sensitive insidious purpose. His urgency was tempered with such tenderness that it was impossible not to believe him when he spoke of love for her. She allowed herself the joy of clasping his strong shoulders, following the line of his back, glorying in the power that lay tensed under her hand.

'I love you, Armando . . .' She felt his sudden stillness, heard the breath rasp in his throat. The words tumbled from her lips in a confession of need. 'I have done for a long time. I'm not sure when—from before we were married, I think, though I didn't realise it. Then, when you put your ring on my finger, and afterwards that night . . . I tried to tell you . . .'

'*Dios!*' he moaned. 'And I was so sure it was still Rico.'

'No,' she said softly but firmly, 'not Rico. You, my darling, only you . . .'

'But you turned me down, pushed me away . . .' It was as if he were afraid she might do so again. Feverishly bright, his eyes scanned her face. 'Was it to punish me for what I did to your wedding dress—ah, Pavane, what did you expect when you taunted me with the thought of your marrying another man? I could have strangled you at that moment!'

'It nearly broke my heart,' she admitted with a little sob. 'I was going to treasure it for the rest of my life, but that wasn't the reason. I couldn't let you love me, Armando. I thought you only wanted me because Isabella had refused to wait and Pablo was leaving the country. You made me feel so cheap when you asked me to name my price.' Still she dared not tell him about Melody, winging a silent prayer that it would never be necessary.

'I tried to buy you, *querida*, because I thought your heart was lost to Rico. What purpose was there in speaking of love?'

Her mouth was dry, her skin flushed, her nerves tingling. It was impossible to be so close to him and not be aware of the powerful forces which raged through his finely-tuned body. 'Oh, my darling,' her arms wound round his shoulders, her ungiven body begged his indulgence, 'I'll never push you away again as long as I live!'

'Wait . . .' His husky voice promised her the world as he swung his legs off the bed, pulling his shirt undone with rough uncaring fingers, tearing if off to reveal the smooth satin skin, the strong muscles of his lean back.

Pavane shuddered, agonisingly aware of the profound stirring deep inside her, watching with intense pleasure as Armando stripped naked. As he shed the last garment she slid her own legs off the bed, pushing the wide neck of her nightdress past her shoulders and breasts, allowing it to fall in a heap at her feet. This time he should be in no doubt as to how much she wanted him.

For a few seconds they stood looking at each other, admiration, need, hunger, mounting to a crescendo between them. Then with a small gasping sob, Pavane went into his arms to be lifted against him, kissed, carried, her mouth locked to his, finally to subside once more on the bed with his lean length on top of her.

'You're so very beautiful, my Pavane . . .' There was wonder and a tremulous joy in the heavy-timbred voice.

'So are you, my darling,' she whispered, discovering for herself the secrets of his body, as his gentle hands stroked her sensitive quivering flesh.

He loved her slowly and with infinite patience, sensing her needs and reservations. Anxious to please him, she offered herself without thought of achieving any satisfaction other than the reward of his pleasure. She had never imagined the way he would control his own urgent needs to her slower rhythm, but with each tender caress, each delicate stroke of his hand and mouth on her soft body he kindled a dormant sensuality, flaming it into a burning inferno of longing.

Instinctively she returned his caresses, knowing by his strangled gasps and moans of pleasure when she most excited him, feeling the fine pitch of his body trembling towards breaking point—and she knew the time was right.

Sobbing his name aloud, spasming beneath his predatory weight, she begged Armando to love her. All her life she would recall the aching beauty of his face, the black hair lying in damp curls on his forehead, beads of sweat glistening above his eyebrows, his mouth slack and swollen, voluptuous and voracious.

'Please,' she breathed, 'oh, please . . . my love . . .'

He came to her in that first instance with skill and gentleness, a perfect unison of interlocking bodies, and in that shuddering moment of stillness before the storm, even while she gloried in feeling he was truly a part of her, he sensed the barrier of her purity and moaned like a soul in Hell.

Every nerve and fibre inside her screamed! If he left her now she would die. There was no way left to protect Melody. She'd taken a fifty-fifty gamble and lost.

Time seemed frozen in that dreadful fraction of a second, but it was merely the flicker of an eyelid while Armando fought to regain rational thought. A mere micro-second before Pavane took the initiative. Arching her body sharply upwards she took the final decision away from Armando. She gave herself to him in the most active, most positive way possible, crying out in blind triumph as she made their union complete.

Fingers assaulting the warm brown skin of his shoulders, points digging deep so fervent her emotion, she sobbed against him, 'Don't leave me, for pity sake don't leave me...' She'd have to face the consequences, but afterwards, please God, afterwards . . .

She felt him move, felt the thrusting beauty of his body begin the ritual of total love. Through the huskiness of passion she heard the tremble of amusement. 'As if I could, *querida*!'

Slowly they climbed down from the peak. Pavane lay cradled in warm, sun-browned arms, her legs intertwined with Armando's golden thighs, her hand against his thudding heart. Only the thinnest shimmer of sweet, musky sweat lay between their two bodies, pulses beating as one, breathing mingled.

His silence was ominous, then without warning he crushed his mouth down on hers making her wilt beneath the fierce assault. She recognised an element of punishment, raising troubled eyes to meet the dark mirrored pools of his, gazing down at her through the fronds of his heavy lashes.

'Rico was never your lover!' It was a cry of triumph and unmistakable joy. 'Not Rico, not your English boy-friend, no one! You've never known another man! Dear God, Pavane, you lied to me. You and Rico lied to me!'

She flinched away from the harsh anguish of that cry. 'Please don't be angry with me,' she beseeched. 'I love you so much, I can't bear to lose you. I prayed you'd never find out I'd lied. I never meant to deceive you . . .' The words faded, her voice shaking as she closed her eyes, not daring to face him for fear of what she might read on his face.

'It was Melody, I suppose? Rico and Melody, and somehow you were made to take the blame for what *they* did, hmm?' His voice was level. With unerring accuracy he had guessed the truth as she had always known he must.

Now she told him the whole story, her face trapped somewhere between his chin and the pillow, her muffled words holding nothing back. She tried to keep her voice from breaking, but towards the end of the recital she couldn't stop her tears falling.

'What will you do?' She forced herself to raise her

head and look at him, desperately trying to measure
his mood from the brooding expression of his dark
eyes, the proud curving mouth and stubborn chin.

'You haven't left me any options. There's only one
thing I can do.'

She felt the blood drain from her face. 'Armando, I
beg you ...'

'There's no need to beg, *amada mia, adorada
mia* ...' Lean fingers trailed down her cheek, their
passage followed by his soft mouth. 'I'm determined
to make up for all the lost time, the lost pleasure this
absurd farce has cost us.'

She could read amusement, affection and the revival
of desire in that dark voice, and dared to hope.

'And Melody?' she whispered.

'I hope she and Rodrigo will have a long, contented
union, blessed with many children.' He lowered his
head to kiss her breast: to suckle the nipple which rose
to his pleasure.

'And Rico?' she dared to ask.

'I imagine he has already learned his lesson one way
or another.' His fingers conjured a subtle magic from
her responsive skin.

'And me?' Pavane asked tremulously. She was very
much his wife by false pretences, and that might be
unforgivable despite what had just happened between
them. 'I'm not what you thought I was.' She couldn't
hide her anxiety. 'What about me?'

'You?' he said, his smile tenderly amused. 'On the
contrary, Pavanita, you're everything I always knew
you were: generous, compassionate, loving ...' His
voice trembled against her sensitive ears, 'And more,
my lovely girl—much, much more.' He kissed the tip
of her nose, seemingly unaware of the dangerous
reactions his wandering hands continued to arouse.
'And you've already paid the penance for your sins.'
There was a deep abiding satisfaction in his words

which he made no attempt to hide. 'It's not every day a girl surrenders her purity.'

'Such a small penance?' She dared to tease him, and then she remembered, holding off his caresses, her tone deepening with excitement. 'Elena!' she gasped. 'Oh, *querido*, I've found out that it was *Elena* that Miguel loved. I was . . .'

Dimly she heard the warm laughter in Armando's voice, slurred with passion. 'Later, my darling, tell me later . . .'

He moved on top of her, his mouth quelling her. As her body yielded, soft and warm and hungry to enjoy him, she could feel him hard and wanting again. He was right. Miguel had waited sixty years to be vindicated, another hour would make little difference.

'Isn't Pavvy feeling well?' Pablo eyed the tray laid for breakfast suspiciously. 'She generally comes downstairs for breakfast, and much earlier than this!' The kitchen clock showed the time at ten-thirty.

'Of course she's well, child.' Ana placed two red roses in a silver vase and put it on the tray. 'She's just tired after staying up so late to see the fireworks.'

'But I stayed up late and I'm not tired,' the boy protested.

'But then you're younger than Doña Pavane, *no*?'

'I suppose so.' Pablo was bored and it showed. 'Is Tio Armando tired, too?' He looked at the tray, his keen eyes observing that it was laid for two.

'He must be.' Ana looked at him reprovingly. 'After driving back through the night. Why, he's hardly had any sleep at all! Enrico was very surprised to see his car outside the garage when he went to collect the post this morning.'

'But I want to *do* something with Pavvy . . .' Pablo

wasn't normally a fractious child, and Ana realised it was only his devotion to the lady of the house that was making him so querulous.

'I fancy you have a rival for her attentions this morning, *chico*,' she said, not unkindly, turning abruptly as the kitchen door was pushed open with some force to reveal Perico.

'Do I smell coffee, Ana?' He gave the housekeeper a winning smile. 'Just what I need!'

'I'll bring it out to you on the patio, Don Perico, if you'll be patient.'

'Esteban's come over with me,' he volunteered, his quick dark eyes flicking across to the breakfast tray as his mouth curled into a smile of satisfaction.

'Will you be staying here again, Don Perico?' Ana asked hopefully. She was fond of her employer's young brother and had looked forward to his presence in the house.

His slim fingers touched the edges of the rosebuds. 'I wasn't too sure about that yesterday,' he murmured softly, 'but yes, now I rather think I will.'

'Can you do something with me, Tio Rico?' Pablo beseeched his young uncle. 'Pavvy's not come down yet and I'm bored!'

'Oh, I think I can arrange something . . .' Perico opened the kitchen door. 'Come in, Esteban, *amigo mio*—what say we all go out for a ride this morning?'

'That's fine with me.' Esteban walked into the kitchen, causing Ana to draw in her breath in exasperation.

'We'll saddle up Zarina for you, I think, my lad. How about that?'

'Oh, yes!' Pablo was beside himself with joy. 'Do you really mean it?' He looked down at his legs. 'You think I've grown enough?

'I think so.' Perico grinned at him. 'It's just a matter of time, *chico*. Everything in its time, its season. It's just a matter of waiting . . .'

'You sound more like a farmer than a physician!' Esteban's youthful smile chided his friend.

'And I'd hoped to sound like a philosopher!'

'Don Perico—*please*!' Ana had to force her way between the three young men to reach the tray.

'Okay—we're off!' Perico gave Esteban a friendly push towards the door, grabbing Pablo round the shoulders and drawing him towards the exit.

Listening to their voices raised in friendly altercation, Ana smiled. She hadn't been unaware of the icy barrier that had seemed to exist between the owner of the Cortijo, whom she loved and respected, and the young English girl he had wed, with her unassuming beauty and friendliness—whom she admired. Nor had she been unaware of the fact that they slept in separate beds in separate rooms.

She regarded the tray with its orange juice, croissants, coffee, its soft sweet buns, its peach jam and its roses with great pleasure and satisfaction, as elated now as she'd been when the Señor's voice, glowing with a splendid happiness, had ordered it to be sent to his wife's room for both of them!

Carefully she negotiated the narrow passageway. She must remember to check the results of the National Lottery when she had a chance.

On such a day a miracle could happen.

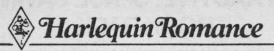

Harlequin Romance

Coming Next Month

2791 HUNTER'S SNARE Emily Ruth Edwards
Faking an engagement to protect her boss from an old flame
seems an outrageous idea for a secretary—until she needs
protection of her own from Connecticut's most dynamic
new businessman.

2792 IMPRESSIONS Tracy Hughes
A Manhattan image consultant has trouble finding the right
look for the host of the TV network's new public affairs show.
Her client thinks he's just fine the way he is—for the network
and for her!

2793 SEPARATE LIVES Carolyn Jantz
Their financial problems were solved by marriage, and love
was an added bonus. Now doubts and the very contract that
brought them together threaten to drive them apart.

2794 CALL OF THE MOUNTAIN Miriam MacGregor
The faster an editor completes her assignment, the faster she
can leave behind a New Zealand station and her boss's
ridiculous accusations. If only his opinion of her wasn't
so important....

2795 IMPULSIVE CHALLENGE Margaret Mayo
When a secretary, who has no illusions about her "love 'em and
leave 'em" boss, finds herself jealous of his glamorous
neighbor, she's shocked. She's fallen in love—the thing she
vowed never to do again.

2796 SAFARI HEARTBREAK Gwen Westwood
This mother doesn't object to her son's yearly visits to his
father, until her mother-in-law's illness forces her into making
the trek back to Africa—scene of her greatest heartbreak...her
greatest happiness.

Available in October wherever paperback books are sold, or
through Harlequin Reader Service.

In the U.S.
P.O. Box 1397
Buffalo, N.Y.
14240-1397

In Canada
P.O. Box 2800, Postal Station A
5170 Yonge Street
Willowdale, Ontario M2N 6J3

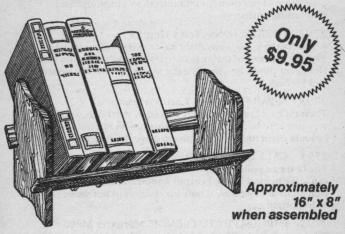

Where passion and destiny meet . . . there is love

Jesse's Lady
Veronica Sattler

Brianna Deveraux had a feisty spirit matched by that of only one man, Jesse Randall. In North Carolina, 1792, they dared to forge a love as vibrant and alive as life in their bold new land.

Available at your favorite bookstore in SEPTEMBER, or reserve your copy for August shipping. Send your name, address, zip or postal code with a check or money order for $5.25 (includes 75¢ for postage and handling) payable to Worldwide Library Reader Service to:

 PLEASE SPECIFY BOOK TITLE WITH YOUR ORDER.

JES-H-1

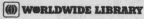

HARLEQUIN HISTORICAL

Explore love with Harlequin in the Middle Ages, the Renaissance, in the Regency, the Victorian and other eras.

Relive within these books the endless ages of romance, set against authentic historical backgrounds. Two new historical love stories published each month.